SHANGHAI ALLEY

SHANGHAI ALLEY

JIM CHRISTY

Ektasis Editions

Canadian Cataloguing in Publication Data

Christy, Jim
   Shanghai Alley

   ISBN 1-896860-10-9

      1. Chinatown (Vancouver, B.C.)—Fiction. I. Title.
   PS8555.H74S52   1997   C813'.54   C97-910234-0
   PR9199.3.C4985S52   1997

© Jim Christy, 1997.
Cover Art: M. Spira

Lyrics to *Say Hello to Love*, © Jim Christy,Down Under Music
(Sydney Australia, 1990)

The translation of the Francois Villon poem is by Lewis Wharton
(*The Collected Poems of Francois Villon*, J.M. Dent & Sons, 1946.)

Published in 1997 by:
Ekstasis Editions Canada Ltd.   **Ekstasis Editions**
Box 8474, Main Postal Outlet   Box 571
Victoria, B.C. V8W 3S1   Banff, Alberta T0L 0C0

Shanghai Alley has been published with the assistance of a grant
from the Canada Council and the Cultural Services Branch of British Columbia.

for

Phil Surguy

Chapter One

"**C**lose!" says the woman urgently "I'm close!"
"Yeah?" says the man, playfully taunting. "Oh, yeah?"

Rrrraaarrnnnggg!

"Damn!" The man looks at the metal alarm clock which is so loud, so heavy that it shudders and its own vibrations move it across the bedside table.

"Now, Gene. Now, Baby! Bring it!"

The man groans. "Ummm."

Rrrraaarrnnnggg! goes the alarm clock.

"That's it! Yes! Oh, Gene. Oh, God!"

Half a minute later, the man reaches over and shuts off the alarm just as the clock approaches the edge of the scarred wood. What with the two bells on top flanking the clapper, and the wind-up key at the side, it occurs to the man in bed that the clock resembles a fat insect which at that moment is staring over a cliff and down to the jungle of floral patterns that make up the carpet.

"Great timing, eh?" says the woman, pulling the sheet up

to her shoulders. The man is on his back now at her side. They both look as if they've been around the block a time or two.

"Yeah," he answers. "You and that clock got the timing down real good."

"Is that a lack of faith I detect?"

The woman pulls the sheet down again, to just below her nipples.

"See! Don't I always blush red? Well? Don't I? It's the foolproof sign. I can't get away with anything, even if I was that type. Course a fellow's got to be in the know."

"Uh huh. But you are an actress."

"Not that good an actress, honey."

She lights a cigarette and smiles. There are the faintest lines about her eyes and mouth. She's about forty years old, a good-looking woman who used to be almost beautiful.

"I'm expected to trust an actress, and one who's been in the carney, no less."

"You been making like you trust me now for what? Eleven years?"

She reaches out a painted fingernail and traces the path of the scar like a waxing moon on his cheek.

"And look who's talking about being a carney," she continues. "When I was just starting out as a kooch girl in Baker's Wonder Shows, who was talking the front in the Ten-In-One, and, I might add, having it off with the tattooed lady?"

"No idea what you're talking about. What kind of company were you keeping, anyhow?"

"It was the company I was trying to keep from keeping."

The man laughed. "Everybody on the lot was after you, Louise, I remember it right. Everybody on the front end and the back end after your rear end."

"What was that painted bitch's name? I forget."

"Hell you do."

"Lotta. Lotta, the tattooed lady. Truth to tell, if it wasn't for her, I might never have noticed you."

8

"What're you talking about?"

"I never told you this before. Reason I gammed on you. I mean with everybody promoting me, it was hardly more than a bunch of faces with bulges in the front of their trousers. You all looked alike to me at first, patch or pinhead, roughie or ride boy, no matter. Took weeks for me to distinguish. Well this one night I'm in the trailer, one of the first travel trailers ever made—that Joe St. Louis, I got to hand it to him, he didn't pinch pennies, just fannies—anyway, there I am, a young innocent from so far back in the sticks that the boondocks looked like the Big Smoke, from Hardisty actually, and I'm lying in the dark on a goddamned carnival lot and..."

"Stick to the truth here, Louise."

"...And I'm feeling lonesome and scared. I mean, I even had to fend off advances from the geek and the lady with the five-legged horse, and all of a sudden the calmness of the night is rent by a piercing screech."

"Oh, my. I believe I know where this is headed."

"At first, I didn't realize what it was. Then I got hep. It wasn't a siren going off, a five-alarmer or a Hey Rube! No, sir-ree. It was Lotta the tattooed bitch who kipped in the back of the truck next to the trailer. I couldn't, I tell you, wait until morning to see the cause of all that commotion."

"Say, I got any more cigars left on the bureau over there?"

"And the next morning who should alight from the back of the truck and hop down into the fresh sawdust? And I says to myself, I says, *Him*? The cause of all *that*? Ah, but how was I to know you'd up and leave me for one reason or another, one ship, one war or another. Nicaragua, Jeez!"

"Seemed like a good idea. Me and Red Batson had us some good times. Wonder whatever happened to him?"

"Good times, I bet. Wenching mostly."

"There was some shooting and getting shot at."

"Remember that ballad you taught me, Gene. Let's see:

You might have become their president,
A prosperous man of means.
But a gunboat came and spoiled your game,
With a hundred and ten marines.

"I forget the rest of it."

"He's down and out, and a woman saves him but another guy kills her, and he hunts him down, puts the knife into him then he becomes a morphine addict and after that things get bad."

"Of all the places, Gene. To think you'd prefer Nicaragua to me."

"And what were you doing while I was in Nicaragua?"

"Hedda Gabler. In Mexico City. Which reminds me," says the woman brushing cigarette ash from her chest and looking at the clock. "I am still an actress, of sorts, and I am working with Mandrake the Magician. At least until his new wife Velvet learns the act. And they are to pick me up in half an hour. So, enough of these sweet remembrances. I got to move this rear end which still ain't so bad after all this time, I do say so myself."

With that, the woman, Louise Jones, aka, for the next several days anyway, Louise Latour, rolls from under the sheets, gets out of bed and walks naked across the floor, grabbing a dress from the back of a chair, and disappears into the bathroom.

When she emerged twenty minutes later, the man was standing by the window looking down past the hotel sign and into the street. He was wearing the pants of a blue pin-striped suit, and a sleeveless undershirt, and holding a white shirt in his hand. He was six feet even, about a hundred and eighty pounds, and still muscular. His black hair was combed straight back. He turned to face her. "So how long you going to be gone?"

"Six days."

10

Louise sat on the bed and stuck her right foot into the ball of nylon that she held in both hands. "Start tonight at the Hi-Hat. Four evenings."

She smoothed the stocking over her toes, wriggled her foot, and began unrolling the nylon up her leg.

"Strictly a club act but it's good. He makes me disappear at the most revealing part of my fan dance. Then it's Friday and Saturday nights at the Starlight. No matinee, thank God. Real spooky show. I mean it. Darkened stage, single spot on Leon. Him in black tie and tails. Me in white gown cut way down to here. Kind of gives me a chill when he says, 'Did you ever ask yourself: What are we put here for?' Then he goes, 'Heh, heh, heh!'"

Louise finished hooking the little belts to the tops of her stockings. When she stood, the skirt ended an inch above her knees and her heels were four inches high. She looked over her shoulder at the backs of her legs, and repeated the line, "What are we put here for? Heh, heh heh!"

"Hey, Gene. Are my seams straight?"

"Yeah. I don't know why the rest of us were put here," he said, grabbing his suit jacket from a hanger in the closet. "but you, sweetheart, were put here to wear high heel shoes."

"Flattery will get you anything that's left to be got. But it'll have to wait six days. Let's go, he's meeting me at the curb."

Only eight-thirty of a May morning and Cordova Street was wide awake and on the hustle. Emerging from the open doorway under the creaking sign for the Rose Hotel, Castle looked both ways and yawned. Japanese men were unloading crates of fish from the rear end of a stake truck just in from Steveston. Half a block away in the other direction, half a dozen Indians were seated in the bleachers at the small, empty ballfield looking toward the pitcher's mound as if at a game only they could see.

As Castle glanced that way a brand new black La Salle appeared out of the background and eased to the curb lane.

11

Behind the wheel, he recognized the handsome features and stylish waxed black moustache of the magician, Leon Mandrake.

"Gene!" When the man smiled, sunlight seemed to glitter off his gold-capped teeth.

Castle patted the fender of the big car. "Doing all right for an old spook worker, eh Leon?"

"Just a poor man's Cadillac, Gene. Hear you had some trouble in Africa."

"Little."

"Hear they got a guy over there in Abyssinia calls himself Akim the Great, walks through fire. Don't reckon you got a chance to catch his act."

"No, I was pretty busy."

"Oh. Hey, I want you to meet my wife, Velvet."

Castle exchanged greetings with the beautiful, fragile woman with long raven hair who was seated next to the magician.

"Well we better get going. Need one rehearsal down in Seattle. Say, Gene, I hear Tiny Penny needs an advance man, you're interested in going back to the carney."

"Thanks for the tip, Leon. But, no, I'm self-employed now."

"So I hear. You take care of yourself, pardner."

Castle put his arm around Louise's waist and opened the back door for her. "Break a leg, kid."

"I'll miss you." She winked, closed the door and the La Salle drove off down Cordova Street.

Chapter Two

For a full minute Castle stood on the sidewalk and considered walking east, having breakfast in the neighborhood, watching the invisible ball game, and generally loitering until the track opened. Considered not going to work, in other words. The customers had not, afterall, been lined up at the office waiting for him to put in an appearance. There had been only two of them in five weeks. But if he did not go to the office today, he might as well chuck the idea and never go which would mean he'd have to get into some other line, and he knew damn well where that had a habit of leading.

So, what the hell, Castle headed west and there was Manny's Good Junk between the Japanese fish market and a Chinese green grocer. Manny himself, with sleeves rolled up, was cranking down his awning. "Miracle of miracles, Mr. Castle. There is sunshine now. But it won't last til lunch, I'll lay you ten to one."

Castle grinned, waved at the fat, bald man and continued on. He looked, out of habit, in the window of the photo shop with its wedding shots, baby pictures, retouched cameos that might have dated from the dawn of the craft. He needed only to glance from the window to the street itself, to realize what an accurate commentary was the photographer's display.

Every race, creed, colour and nationality had a representative out here. You need to decipher a letter in farsi, just hold on and the right person will be along before the light changes. Have to locate a four hundred pound Turkish gentleman to play snake charmer in your amateur theatrical presentation, you'll find him across the street shooting eight-ball at the back of Basil's Respectable Billiards.

Up ahead near the corner of Main Street, the most exhausted horse in the world, pulling a milk wagon, came to a stop alongside an Auburn Speedster. The spavined nag was too tired to swat flies with his tail. His blinders hid the shiny car, the owner of which, Big Lou Runnells, stepped from a doorway and flipped a silver dollar to a wino with one foot bare, the other in high-top caulk boot.

Turning the corner, Castle saw a group of people gathered in the middle of the sidewalk outside the Rio Hotel. There was a squad car and an unmarked blocking traffic. A constable was shooing away onlookers. As he approached, Castle could make out, between the legs of the curious, and on the ground, a body. A newspaper covered the man's face. Raising his gaze, Castle recognized Horace Koronicki. Another cop in a suit was saying things to him, and Koronicki was staring at the dead man, nodding absently.

He looked up when Castle came near. "Male caucasian," he said to him. "Cause of death: gunshot wound to the chest. Suspect in custody, name of Juney Mance."

The detective bent down and lifted a corner of the newspaper.

"Henry the Hype," Castle said.

14

There was a newspaper reporter, a short guy, hat pushed back on his head, taking all this in, scribbling furiously on his stenographer's pad.

"Henry Arnold Harris. Age thirty-seven." Koronicki let go of the paper. His face flushed red as he straightened up. "And I'd say about a decade over-do."

"It's tough times, Detective."

"It's always those kind of times in this business, Castle. As you should know."

Castle nodded at Koronicki and glanced at the man with him. This detective chewed gum and shot back the hard look for no possible reason save innate contrariness. Castle sighed and walked on.

At Carrall and Pender, he turned into Ramona's Deluxe Cafe, almost tripping over a battered valise by the coatrack. As he nudged it away with his foot, Castle noticed it was decorated with a sticker from a CP hotel in the Rockies, a reminder of someone's better days.

In the first booth to the right and along the wall, a guy in a flashy suit leaned across the table, rubbed his thumb back and forth across his fingertips, advising his companion, a seventeen year old girl with seventy year old eyes, that she'd better dig real deep and come up with more, much more, moo-la.

At the counter across the way, a tiny blonde massaged her feet and drank coffee, switching hands, switching feet.

"Little Flo. Just get off?"

"Hi, Gene. Jesus, yeah. Goddamned stag. Feed salesmen or something from the prairies."

Castle took a seat at the other end of the counter and ordered coffee and a sinker from Maude. In back of him, a couple of old Swedes were complaining about a job they'd just come off back in the bush up near Bella Bella. Risking our lives for nothing. On some goddamned gypo show, by jesus. He noticed old Matty Muldoon, face like a boiled lobster, nursing a mug of tea and staring out at the street or at what he could

15

see of it through the steamy window. Seventy-five, he was, if a day. Had called at every port on earth before the city of Vancouver was born. Still wore his seaman's cap.

Guy Roberts, the king of sugar and one of the richest men in the province, sat at his booth as he did every morning with Raymond Thomas, also one of the richest men in the province. The latter, a Negro, pretended to be the former's chauffeur but was actually his partner. The two met several years before on Saltspring one of the Gulf Islands. Thomas' people had been the first settlers on the island back in the middle of the last century, three hundred black people having chartered a boat in San Francisco to flee racial conditions in the home of the free. They landed in Victoria and spread out across the area. Thomas himself had been doing well, buying fish from the boats that called at the island. Guy Roberts was an ambitious but illiterate deckhand on one of the boats. The two men began to pal around.

What they had in common was ambition. Thomas taught Roberts to read and write. These new skills proved the white man's keys to riches. Once Roberts had unlocked the door, he kept it open for his friend. Thomas immediately displayed uncanny skill in choosing good investments. When Roberts moved to the city, Thomas went along as "chauffeur," negro financial advisers being unknown; any kind of negro being virtually unknown.

Six months after they settled in Vancouver, Thomas disappeared for three days and when he surfaced did not look so good. "Been on a toot, eh?" his pal said, knowingly.

"Well," said Thomas, "let's just say I went looking for another negro."

So every six months for twenty years, Thomas had taken three days off to go looking for another negro.

Loggers, sailors, hookers and their pimps, transients, bookies, hustlers, grifters, grafters, and the Sugar King passing time in Ramona's Deluxe Cafe, and none of them knew who in hell Ramona was. Maude didn't know. Matty Muldoon said the place was there when he first came to town in the late-Eighties which made Ramona's older than the Only Seafood Restaurant, and it might even have predated the Seven Little Tailors. The current owner, and cook, Tommy Chew, didn't know and didn't have time to think about it, what with working sixteen hours a day. But he had Ramona, whoever she was, to thank, in part, for putting his number one son through the University of British Columbia, the first oriental graduate.

"Frankly, I'm fed up with Marxism."

Castle could not help but glance over his shoulder to the origin of this confession, a skinny, tousled-haired kid no older—in years, anyway—than the weary-eyed hooker who was holding back. He was talking to a healthier-looking but also tousled kid of the same age who was wearing a suit jacket over a Cowichan sweater. Their school books were between them on the table. "Anarchism's the only hope for the freedom of mankind."

You said it, kid, Castle thought to himself.

Louis Chew thought, he hadn't gone to university to study anarchism. No sir, it was engineering straight down the line. But in these crazy days there seemed to be more future for the kid in the booth. Things might change though.

"Bourgeois adventurism," pronounced his companion. "Anyway, we want to same thing as you do, ultimately. Marx said the state will wither away."

Castle finished the last of his refill, bought two to go in thick cardboard cups.

The newsie at the corner, a middle-aged Indian man, stooped by the hump on his back, saw him coming, grabbed and folded a paper, and held it out.

"So what's the latest?" Castle asked, taking the paper and opening it.

"We're in a Depression, what it says here. And they're starting to get restless over in Spain."

"Any good news?"

"Sunshine's good for my back but it won't last."

"Yeah, Manny Israel told me. Anything else?"

"Only this Baby Yack. Out of Toronto? Stopped Jeffra last night in ten at the Garden."

"Well, that's something."

"Ain't enough. World out here's crazy. I'm going back to the reserve, I think."

Castle looks up from the paper and sees the old couple coming along the other side of Pender Street. The man is bent and bowlegged, lugging a canvas sack, limping, there is a banjo slung by a rope across his back. The woman behind is just as old and just as bent, and she is pulling a wooden wagon loaded with junk. The old man stops and waits, and offers his hand to help her down from the curb. They turn and begin hobbling up the narrow crowded street called Shanghai Alley.

The newsie has also been watching them and Castle nods in their direction. "Maybe only love endures. What d'you think Woody?"

"Tell it to them that's fighting in Spain, Gene. Tell it to my ex-old woman for that matter."

The two old people are swallowed up by the busy street, clogged by pedestrians and push carts, horses, cars and trucks, and crates and cans overflowing with refuse. So narrow is this street that the signs on either side with their Chinese characters almost touch and form a canopy over all this activity. Down at the far end of the short block is a waterfront tavern beyond which can be seen the prow of a ship from someplace far away.

18

Chapter Three

C astle crossed Carrall Street and climbed the six wide steps to the revolving doors of a five-story office building. In an alcove on the right hand side of the marble-floored lobby, a woman was seated in front of a telephone switchboard rapidly plugging and unplugging lines. A small fan near her feet pushed the air around, it had loosened a wisp of her brunette hair and was fluttering the hem of her skirt.

"Just a mo-ment, pul-leeese," she said into the mouthpiece when she noticed Castle standing there. He handed her one of the cups of coffee.

"Ah, thanks. No messages."

"No?" Castle pointed to a dozen or so little squares of paper skewered on a thin spike at the side of the switchboard. "Who're all those for?"

"You got to ask?" the woman said, brushing at the stray lock of hair. "Your next door neighbor—Christ, this coffee's good—the bookie, most of them."

"I'm in the wrong business, Laura."

"Sure are. Hey, what're you looking at?"

"I'm hoping a big breeze is going to come up."

"Hummphf! You ever get a decent job, I might let you take me out and have a little peek under there."

"Promises, promises."

As Castle left the switchboard room, he heard Laura saying, "No, he's not in. Awright, I'm not supposed to do this but let's have it. Fifth race?..."

When he reached the second floor, Castle turned and saw, down at the far end of the dim brown hall, a man who was leaning with arms and elbows against his door. Castle stopped for a moment to watch. He took hold of the banister and pulled. The creaking startled the man who dropped his hands to his sides as he turned. One hand held a pencil, the other a piece of paper. Castle began walking toward him, past wood doors with opaque glass windows.

Early thirties, thin, medium height, the man was dressed in the pants from one dark suit and the jacket from another; he had on a flannel shirt, knit tie and clean workman's boots. He might have been a respectable young labourer dressed for a Sunday stroll with the family in Stanley Park, except for the pen and pencils in his jacket pocket, the rimless glasses, the Leon Trotsky-haircut and the symmetrical knot in his tie.

Castle reached his door. Between the two men, gilt lettering on the opaque glass announced

CASTLE
9 AM ------?

"If you're a peeping Tom," said Castle, "You picked the wrong kind of glass to try and look through."

"But I'm..."

"And what kind of guy wants to peep at a man my age anyhow?"

"I resent that. I'm..." the man held up the pencil and a piece of paper torn from a notebook— "I was leaving you a note."

"A mash note?"

The younger man smirked. "I've heard that you'd become cynical but I wish you would please try and stop your clowning."

"Well, pardon me."

"I have come on serious business. And, what is more, you are late. It's nine-fifteen."

Castle sighed. "I'm beginning to think maybe I got here too early."

"My name is Martin Finnegan and I have a job for you."

Castle reached for the doorknob. "In that case, I suppose you should come in."

The waiting room was contained within a few square feet and separated from the office proper by a cheap pine partition that rose three quarters of the way to the ceiling. Privacy not, therefore, being an issue, Castle had replaced a flimsy door with a beaded curtain. He'd put a Chinese lacquered screen and a hardbacked chair on either side of the doorway. A nice touch, the screens, Castle liked to tell himself, too bad the crowds were missing it.

Finnegan, fumbling with the beads, followed him into the office. Directly across the room was a heavy wooden desk before a bank of three windows that offered a wide rooftops-and-chimneys vista. The windowsill was a bookcase, the books being several volumes of the encyclopedia, the bookends being bricks, each holding a partially filled bottle, one of rye, one of dark rum.

There was a wooden chair on either side of the desk and a wicker two-seater along the right-hand wall. If enough people ever penetrated the inner sanctum, one or two of them could sit on the wicker and look across the room at an wildebeest-antler hat rack and a Dahomey mask above the rack. This

21

elongated face stared back across the room at the rounded visage of a Haida transformation mask above the wicker chair.

Otherwise the walls were decorated with framed photographs; a couple of these were of horses crossing finish lines; one of them was of Haile Selassie; others featured prize fighters or other kinds of men who fought but with guns and ostensibly for justice and equality, or something. In some of these latter pictures, one man or another had an arm slung over Gene Castle's shoulders.

"What I want to talk to you about is..."

"Wait a second," said Castle. "It's not official until I sit behind my desk and you in the clients's seat."

Finnegan smirked but did what was indicated. Before him was a jade hippopotamus who displayed an open mouth stuffed with wooden matches. Next to the animal, a woman of curvaceous purple glass held a brass ashtray above her head.

The rest of the desk top was covered by a blotter, pen and pencil set, an opened book of the encyclopedia, and a tray that held a pitcher of water and two glasses.

"Who's your decorator?"

Castle thought the young man kind of sniffed when he asked the question.

"Firm of Johnson Johnson and Shoor."

"What?"

"Osa and Martin Johnson and Toots Shoor."

"Oh. Uh..."

"I can understand why you looked confused. I was too. Don't see why it took three of them myself. Anyway..."

"I'm from the Workers' Union Alliance," Finnegan said exasperatedly. "A touchy situation has developed and certain parties have recommended you."

"I'm flattered."

"But after experiencing your sarcasm, I'm not so sure they made the proper decision."

"Then why don't you battle your way back through the

beads and debate the matter with yourself."

"Now see here, Castle. I was reluctant to come here at all but due to the peculiar nature of the case..."

"Listen, pal. Skip the preamble. As you can see, I'm a busy man." Castle reached behind him and grabbed one of the bookend bottles. "There're only two empty chairs in the waiting room and I got all these expensive furnishings to pay off. I got half this bottle of demerara rum to finish, half the bottle of rye and all of book fourteen of the Encyclopedia Britannica to read."

"The strike fund of the Workers' Union Alliance is missing. Twenty thousand dollars."

"Call the coppers."

"Don't be silly."

"Sorry."

"The publicity would ruin us. They'd notify the papers and we would be thoroughly discredited. Right now we have a city-wide, hopefully province-wide, general strike in the makings. The press being handmaiden of the bosses would conspire to make us look ridiculous."

"Then go to a legitimate private investigator."

"Those people are all ex-cops, as you're well aware. That is why we have come to you."

"On account of I'm an *ill*egitimate private investigator?"

"That, of course, but more because of your background. Even though you have given up the Struggle. Let down the Cause."

"The cause let down me. By the way, young man, I believe I detect in your voice capital letters and disdain."

"If there is disdain it is no match for your cynicism. We are hoping that whatever sympathies you may retain are still with those who fight on. My information has it that you held an IWW card as a youth and that you fought with Sandina, escaping Nicaragua after the US Marines invaded. Only a short time ago you were running guns to Ethiopia. Then..."

"Yeah, I know all that."

"Then you fought for the Partisans against the Italian invaders."

Castled nodded his head and pointed to an eight-by-ten photograph on the wall. "Yeah, and the Lion of the Desert was so grateful, he gave me that autographed picture and no assistance when Graziani's boys captured me. Let's see, twenty-five dollars a day and expenses will do it. Legitimate expenses; within reason, of course."

"Twenty-five dollars a day? That's outrageous!" Finnegan exclaimed. "We were thinking that, because of your past, you would..."

"Do it for free? You kidding? There's a Depression going on, the newsie just told me."

"Yes, there surely is a Depression going on, and the rights of the workers are being oppressed at every turn. There is so much at stake that you could at least take the assignment for expenses. And you can't be doing all that badly. Why that encyclopedia there is brand new, the Coronation edition. I know how much that costs. A couple of months wages to a working man. It sits unread in every *au courrant haute bourgeois* living room."

"Step closer, folks. Ties a Windsor knot and speaks French with an eastern public school accent. *Oui, mec.* The Coronation edition. But if you look real close, you'll see that I only got half the set. Up to book fourteen, 'Libido to Mary, Duchess of Burgundy.' You see, there was this beautiful woman give it to me. I remember her fondly. I was summoned to her quaint *pied-a-terre* in Shaughnessy Heights. A guy in a funny suit and a mug with a limited repertoire took my hat. This dame wanted me to find out the name of the doxie for whom her hubby was playing big butter and egg man. I happened to see this set of encyclopedias and, goodness knows what possessed me, Martin Finnegan, I suddenly heard myself asking, in lieu of a fee, for half the set as a retainer. The rest to be delivered on completion of the assignment. Well, I discovered who the old coot was seeing but almost simultaneously my client herself was killed in a boating accident along with her lover--Manny Chung, of all people. Guy who used to run the Tai Paw games over there underneath Shanghai Alley. Maybe you read about it? Alas, I never got the second half of the set although I have filed a writ of attachment on the estate. Twenty-five dollars a day, Mr. Finnegan. And expenses; within reason, of course."

"All right, all right," Finnegan said, resignedly. "We have no alternative."

"Otherwise, you wouldn't be here. Now, tell me, where did you keep the money? Underneath a pile of placards?"

"I suppose this is the real you and not just a jaded veneer?"

"On the other hand, maybe it is a veneer to distract you from taking notice of a heart broken by lost illusions."

"I doubt it."

"Talk about cynicism. The money, pal."

"It was kept in a safe in a locked closet in an office at the hall. Now let me tell you my thoughts on the crime. Given our precautions, it was obviously committed by a crime professional. A thief hired by the bosses, or even a cop."

"Uh huh. Look, do you have any pep rallies scheduled at your union hall?"

"There is a meeting tonight at eight, if that's what you mean. But it's for members only."

"And how does one become a member?"

"One pays the dues."

"And does one receive a ring with a secret compartment containing a photo of Uncle Joe Stalin amid proud peasant children? Don't answer that. I'd like to meet the members so I'll see you at eight."

"But surely you're not implying that it might be an, an..."

"Inside job's the expression in the parlance of the under world."

"Why that is preposterous."

"It's a preposterous world, Mr. Finnegan."

"The WUA is one big union. Stealing from all of us is the same as stealing from one of us."

"That's right and it works out to more money that way."

"But, but...."

The young man stammered and Castle poured himself another drink.

"See you tonight, Finnegan. Unless you want to stay and join me in a wee shot? I'll tell you all about this dinner party I attended in Addis Ababa. Selassie was at the head of the table, naturally, and I was on his right. Across from me sat a young Italian fellow, handsome in a brutish way, he was. His business was running guns, same as mine. The lion was buying from him—the enemy—same as from me—the allie. How bout that, eh? In order to get the guns from the Italian gent, the hero of his people had to agree to certain concessions. You want to stick around, my hardy, I'll tell you what those concessions were."

Finnegan stood, pushed the chair away abruptly and walked out of the room. Castle heard the door slam as he picked up the encyclopaedia volume from his desk. He took a sip of his rum and began to read: "Libido. Defined by Freud as 'the energy of those instincts which have to do with all that may be comprised under the word Love.'"

Chapter Four

A stout woman of late middle age sat tapping her pencil, watching the last union members file into the meeting hall. Her feet in heavy shoes were crossed at the ankles under the table. Before her, arranged just so, were stacks of papers, piles of pamphlets, a logbook and donation box. Looking through the opened doors at the men and women talking in little groups or finding their seats, she told herself that tonight's meeting should prove exciting. That young man was sure to stir things up, a rabble-rouser that one, reminded her of the heady days and nights before the War. A heavy accent intruded on her thoughts.

"Pardon me, lady."

He stood in grey work pants and shirt, cloth cap, scuffed boots and a long denim jacket such as a trainman might wear.

"Oh, yes, how can I help you?"

"Thank you." He whipped the cap from his head and held it before him rolled up in both hands. "I would like to make membership with the WUA union."

"That's fine then. Are you employed?"

"Who is employed these days?" said the man shrugging his shoulders.

The woman smiled gently. "Membership for the unemployed is fifty cents, if you can afford it, that is."

"I have saved the money." From his baggy pants pocket, he brought out a small cloth change purse with a metal clasp.

A man with a bony, weather-beaten face glanced at him on his way to lean in the doorway and smoke the last of a hand rolled cigarette.

"Here is money."

"Thank you," she said, taking the coins. "And what is your name?"

"Leon Salinsuk."

She pushed the log book toward him. "Would you sign, please. You're Polish? Lithuanian?"

The man raised himself to his full stature, and proudly said, "I am Ukrainian," he said proudly. "From same town as Makno."

The woman smiled again. She had a nice, easy smile. She began selecting sheets of paper from the different piles.The man in the doorway dropped his butt to the floor, crushed it with the toe of a boot wrapped with electrician's tape and looked again at the man signing the book. His eyes narrowed.

"Say, Gene? Castle, is that you?"

The woman behind the desk looked from one man to the other. The new member of the WUA had not seemed to notice the voice.

"Please take this literature. Can you read English?"

"Yes. But not so good."

"Uh, sorry pal," said the gaunt weather-beaten man. The new member glanced at him and resumed taking the pamphlets that the woman handed him.

The other man turned and walked into the hall.

"And do you speak Russian?"

28

"Of course, what you think?"

"Fine, fine. Then here are some things to read in Russian. Glad to have you with us in the struggle, comrade. Hurry in now. The meeting has just begun."

The man put his cap back on and touched the brim. "Thanking you, comrade Lady."

All the seats in the hall were occupied except for some in the last two rows. The new member took one of these and looked toward the front of the room where a stocky man was speaking at a lectern on the dais. Behind him, others, including Finnegan, sat at a table. There were posters on the walls; two men with shirts open to show their barrel chests, a woman holding a gun, all of them with noble visages, staring resolutely at a golden horizon, under the legend "Fight Fascism." Another showed two massive sinewy forearms with thick wrists and block-like hands squeezing the life out of a rotund, bald-headed man, obviously a boss.

The speaker was in his late fifties with a thatch of grey hair and tufts of eyebrows who was built like the stump of a Douglas fir or, rather, like one of the workers on a poster. He was Harry Greene, a guy who had learned his politics in the bush and on the fishing boats.

"I promised to keep this brief, comrades. So I'll finish up by saying that the loss of our strike fund should have no detrimental effect on our enthusiasm and dedication but it must cause us to pause temporarily, and I stress the word 'temporarily,' in our great plans in order to take stock of the situation. A general strike at this time is not only ill-advised but it might prove disastrous. We have been robbed of our ability to sustain those who will be making the greatest sacrifice. Remember a general strike is not itself the goal. The goal is better conditions for all workers. We should turn our attention, and devote our energies, to devising new strategies for bringing about those conditions. I thank you."

Harry Greene sat down to steady if unexuberant applause

29

from about half the crowd.

"Gene," said a hushed voice. "I knew it was you. It's been a long time."

The man who had been smoking in the doorway took the next seat.

"Hey, how's it going, Frank?"

"Rough hustling, like us in the old days."

"Yeah, the good old days."

"Me, I just hit town."

Another man approached the lectern and began to speak. Frank stuck a cigarette in one side of his mouth and, out of the other, said, "Been seeing the country by sidedoor Pullman. But the last I heard of you, you was supposed to be shaking a jolt in Africa or somewheres."

"Sisters of Mercy sent me a cake with a file in it."

"Must have been Angel's Food."

"Good old Frank."

"So what's with the Russian bit? I didn't know you could speak that stuff but, then again, I remember you was always learning foreign languages."

"I'm working for the One Big Union now."

A man come along the aisle and took the seat on the other side of Frank.

The new member of the WUA struck a match on the seam of his pant leg, held it up to the wiry, hard-bitten man and muttered, "Meet me at the Anchor when this is over."

"Thanks for the light, comrade."

Frank got up and moved off.

"So I ask you, comrades: how long are we to remain bound and chained to old-fashioned notions?"

Castle took a look at the speaker.

"Our esteemed Chairman wants us to 'pause' as he says and 'take stock.' But what I believe is that there is not time to take stock, to discuss this and debate that. And pause? There can be no pause in the fight to end the suffering of the unemployed and the humiliation of the workers who carry the fat cats on their backs."

Jesus, Castle muttered under his breath. The rhetoric never changes. Just for curiosity's sake, he would like to witness that fleeting moment just before a progressive notion becomes an old-fashioned one. There was always somebody tripping on somebody else's heels ready to brand that one outdated, to push him aside and onto the scrap heap of antediluvian ideas. The ironic part, in the left-wing game, was that the words never changed despite new theoretical pronunciamentos from Mother Russia. Oh, yeah, Castle thought glumly, The Union of Soviet Socialist Republics had been another stop on his road of political disillusionment. But he hadn't paused long enough to get caught napping. Sure he had a past and it had made him cynical, just as that Finnegan up there on the dais trying to look important even as he peeks around the water pitcher, had said. But at least he could chart the course of it.

"It is, therefore, high time to get the bosses off our backs."

It may have been rhetoric most hackneyed but plenty of them were giving it their rapt attention, not to mention a cheer now and again as well as the occasional upraised fist. They were on the edge of their seats for this guy.

He was just a couple of years younger than Castle himself but a hell of a lot prettier. Healthy full head of black wavy hair and a smooth olive complexion. Those almond-shaped brown eyes must make the girls swoon, Castle thought, yet they, the eyes, were hard. And despite the refined features, his mouth was downright cruel. Hell, maybe it's the combinations that did it. He could be an aristocrat if it weren't for the way he gestured with his hands, nothing refined about them. And the accent, he couldn't peg it. The guy sounded like one of those people who broadcast to North America from a European country on shortwave, their English just a little too precise.

Castle frowned; none of it added up. Not yet anyway but

31

it always did and when it did, well, when it did it was usually irrelevant.

"So you must ask yourselves what a 'pause' means. A month? Two months? Or three? Three months more of misery and injustice? Ask the comrade who is locked out, inquire of the man sleeping under the bridge. And the woman in the sweatshop, what about her? What of her children begging for a crust of bread? Ask yourselves how long this must go on. I say three *minutes* more is too long. I say let us have a general strike *now*!"

His final words had been punctuated with bursts of excited applause. When he was finished, many of the younger people jumped to their feet, cheering wildly. There were whistles and shouts, stomping of feet and more upthrust fists.

The new member from Ukraine got up too but no one paid him any mind as he headed for the door.

He hung around outside for a half hour watching the rest of them leave. Just another working stiff trying to light the butt of a cigar. He'd ridden the blinds in from the prairies, no hope of anything to do until it was cherry-picking time in the Okanagan. So he leaned against a brickwall and the faded face of a painted cherub who would have you believe that all a fella or a gal had to do was spread a little raspberry jam on a thick slice of bread and everything would be hunky-dory.

They continued to file out, some going off on their own like Frank there; most though in pairs or groups. A bunch of them surrounded the last speaker, several eager young ladies hanging on his words, waiting for a look, and there was Finnegan on the edge of the party, fearful of missing something. The pretty boy threw back his head and opened his mouth and made sounds like laughing, and the rest of them laughed with him.

Over there's Harry Greene in a clutch of old-timers, all bound for the scrap heap. Hey, and those others, the downtrodden, the unemployed and aimless drifters. Some genuine workers. A couple of gents who look like they used to go to the office every day; once had a wife, couple of kids and nice little house and one day it was all gone, and they never knew what hit them. Why, if you used to have a secretary to pinch and a couple of salesmen to boss around, you might get to thinking you're entitled to something better than this, and twenty grand will buy it. Tired of bending over in the mine shaft, tired of riding freights. Twenty Gs would buy a seat in the club car, a mixed drink and a lot of fresh air.

Did that one over there boost the twenty grand? That grey cadaver twisted like a question mark, the one the cane's holding up? Yes, him with an eye full of cataracts and a mouth full of nothing but gums. That tottering nonentity has a name, Buddy Bristol, and he was *old* when he fought in the Spanish-American war—for the Phillipinos—and *older* when he was with Villa in Chihuahua. What did it get him? Why the respect of most all the other old panhandlers who let him have a seat at Pigeon Park whenever he wanted one, that's what. He didn't steal the twenty grand? Well, why the hell not?

Perhaps it was her, the kind lady who took the names and passed out the literature. She has the keys, has locked up, nobody to walk her home. Thirty years devoted to the struggle and what thanks has she received? But, no; there's not a larcenous bone in the old dear's unused body, and nobody to give her a tumble and a turn in the hay. Maybe that polite new fellow from Ukraine, she thinks. Clean him up, give him a shave and press his clothes, well, I could do worse. Times get better, he could find a job, tithe the WUA, get us a cottage in the south-east part of town where there's some clean air to breathe; we could get hitched at a union picnic. —But she's thinking no such thing. She's married already, to the Cause. So the keys go in the handbag and she walks away alone, in stout shoes and thick stockings, back to the flat, the cat and a nice hot mug up.

Chapter Five

The way it looked, thought Castle, was like the two ships were behemoths from a lost world and they had crept up to the wharf and were about to rise out of the water to crush the little tavern that sat unaware in the fog, flashing its blue neon anchor up Shanghai Alley. As he got closer, they turned into just a couple of working stiffs, one waiting to haul grain up the coast to Alaska, the other ready for the big Orient run and loaded with lumber.

There was a circle of white mist around the globe of the pole lamp by Pier Eleven and a smear of light on the pavement in front of the Anchor Club. He pushed open the heavy oak door.

Four seamen at the closest round table looked up at him like he had just surprised them in a corner of the hold conspiring to seize the ship, toss the old man into the foamy brine and turn her around for the Marquesas. "Hiya, mates," Castle said, dispelling the mood.

There were a couple of men playing darts, four others at

cards. A young dark kid, maybe a Mexican who'd jumped ship, was sweeping the floor of wide black-and-white tiles, probably in exchange for a meal and a flop. The tiles got smaller as they climbed halfway up the walls, and above them hung framed photographs of ships, from CP liners to old Clipper ships, a representative collection of those that had called at the port of Vancouver during the last fifty years.

A couple of men in suits were at one table, and Castle pegged them for marine insurance agents. Another guy was in a suit too, only his cost over a hundred dollars and he was wearing spats, no less. Also, he was with a woman who, if she did not have her back turned to the dart game would surely have caused some nasty puncture wounds. Castle did not have to run a mitt camp to discern that this was not a marine insurer out with the missus.

Frank was seated by himself near the middle of the floor, old Johnny at a table along the wall. Frank looked away from the tip of the cigarette that he was holding like he was about to join the dart game, saw Castle and waved him over.

"Hey, pal. Pull up a chair. And what's this you said about working for the Union? You give up knocking around the world, soldiering for freedom and fortune?"

"Yeah, I decided I could get shot at in my own home town just as well. Also me and the local bacteria know each other so well there's no surprises."

Castle called to the old man who was nursing a beer, his banjo leaning against his leg, the glass almost hidden in his thick gnarled fingers. "Hiya, Johnny."

"Lad,"said the old man, showing a couple of yellow teeth and pointing his glass at Castle.

The waiter approached carrying a tray with four drafts, and dragging one foot behind him. Castle's casual expression turned to one of shocked dismay. The little man's upper body was twisted so that one shoulder was up by his ear. He read Castle's look but his expression didn't change, it was too sad

35

already.

"Nice to see you back, Gene."

"Been a long time, Pete."

The man smiled with his deep brown eyes and turned away. Castle watched him in spite of himself.

"It was two years ago," Frank said. "Took a spill at Cour D'Alene."

"He was the best harness driver anybody ever saw out west."

They finished half a beer in silence.

"So what's the gossip on the strike fund?"

Frank shrugged. "Just disappeared. One night it's in the safe; the next, it's not."

"You got any suspicious characters lurking about the group?"

"You kidding? Only about a hundred-fifty of them."

"Any yeggs?"

"Wouldn't be surprised. Got at least one of every other type. One guy claims he's related to Jesus, the first communist. And you need a midget to ride a one-wheeled bicycle on a wire twenty feet up in the air for your niece's birthday party, we got one of those. Rumanian fella."

"Lew Sandulescu?"

"Yeah. You know him?"

"Sure. Used to play still dates with Baker's Super Shows back east."

"Well he got off the wire'n joined the struggle. How about a guy follows the harvest renting out inflatable women?"

"You're funning me now, I hope."

"Think I'd joke about a thing like that? He's got a whole bunch of them. Fat ones, skinny ones, and even a, uh, man doll, looks just like Gary Cooper."

"I don't think I want to hear anymore about it."

"Okay. But the funny part is, he's making good money. Guy from Montreal."

36

"The missing strike fund."

"Fellow that did it, he didn't need a drill or a torch or a stick of dynamite. Didn't even need to use a screwdriver."

"You mean, maybe he just went right, left a full turn past zero and right again?"

"So it would appear but don't be looking at me, old pal, old buddy. Twenty dollars or twenty thousand, I'd just wake up a day, a week or a month later, and it'd all be gone."

"Who's on the executive besides Harry and the guy who thinks he's a movie star? What's his name?"

"Alex Tremaine. Guy like him can get all the doxies he wants, he don't need the money. Man, the women can't leave him alone and he acts like he don't care. Maybe they like that, he's a challenge or something. Who knows. Then there's that Finnegan."

"Anybody else?"

"Just your old buddy, Rose Jenkins but she's sort of honorary lifetime chairman. She's getting on and hasn't been around to the hall in nearly four months. You think it's one of them, maybe? Thing is if it was somebody who already had the combination, you'd think they'd at least whack the safe a few times with a hammer, allay suspicion."

"Stands to reason. Who handles the money? Puts in the dues, takes it out to pay the rent?"

"Finnegan. But if he took it why didn't he run with it?"

"Maybe because if he took it and stayed around everyone would think it can't be him because if it was he'd have taken it and run."

"Yeah. But I'd bet on Rose. Maybe she's going to lam it with the moo-la over to Europe and replace that Simpson dame?"

"Sure, that makes sense. Rose is worth abdicating for."

The tavern door opened and an old woman stood on the threshold, her toothless mouth agape, her eyes squinting.

Castle looked, said, "Hey, Frank, can this be the same

town I left a few short years ago? They letting women in the
bars, sit with the men?"

"Same town. Same laws except for around here. It's
Shanghai Alley, Gene. A world unto itself."

"My Johnny boy in here?" the woman cried in a cracked
voice.

One of the card players muttered to his companions, "Poor
Johnny boy. Ain't no place to hide."

"Johnny, you in here? I don't see so good."

Johnny called to her but the old lady didn't hear.

"Can't see too good, can't hear too good either," said
another of the card players. "Reminds me of an old nag we
had on the ranch when I was a boy. She was too ugly to die
and too mean to ride."

"Here I am, May." The old man called to her again. "Over
here in the corner."

"Some guys'll ride anything," said the other card player.

When her one working eye fixed on her man, the old lady
cackled with pleasure.

"Now there, lads," spoke a sailor, "is the best argument a
man ever had for turning to the booze for forgetting."

"No, boy." One of his companions shook his head. "There
ain't enough booze in the world."

May's legs were like sticks except behind the knees where
veins bunched like clusters of grapes. To Castle, May and
Johnny didn't look any older than when he'd left town a few
years ago. In fact, it was as if they hadn't aged in the twenty
or so years since he first remembered seeing them on the
streets. They'd been ancient way back then.

There was some attempt to stifle guffaws as the old lady
engineered her descent onto the chair across from her man.
Pleated, crinkled and gouged, Johnny's face presented the
room a magnificent scowl. He grabbed his banjo and plucked
at the strings. Then in a voice that might have come from
beyond the fog outdoors, from the stones and barnacles and

old tires at the bottom of the harbour, he began to sing. The first notes cut a sailor's smart remark in mid-phrase so that you half-waited for the punch line, and laughter stopped on a dime.

The card players, the sailors and the marine insurers, the guy with the spats and the girl with the legs, Castle and Frank, studied the puddles of beer on their tables. May wore an expression of hideous bliss as Johnny strummed the banjo, looking into her eyes, singing:

I love you as I loved you
When you were sweet
When you were sweet sixteen.

Chapter Six

Victory Square is a small park on a slope between Hastings and Pender Streets in downtown Vancouver. Grass that the familiar rain keeps green all the year round is bisected by a cement walkway. A cenotaph at the foot of the hill honours those who lost their lives Over There in the War to End All Wars. There are benches along the walkway and Gene Castle sat on one of them reading the newspaper, an overwrought account continued from the front page of a bit of shady land development out in the Fraser River Valley. Business types occupied other benches and other types with no business whatsoever sprawled on the grass. There was an Indian sleeping it off with a half-dead bottle at his side, his shirt was opened and his bulge of stomach was taking in a sun that was appearing for the second consecutive day after spending half a year in hiding.

A man carrying a briefcase came down the hill, and Castle lowered his newspaper.

"Hey Finnegan!"

When he was adjacent to the bench Finnegan stopped and looked upon Castle with evident displeasure.

"I wouldn't want to disturb you. I notice you are hard at work, earning your twenty-five dollars a day. And expenses. You didn't even have the decency to show up at the meeting last night."

"Will there be more?"

"Yes, the missing strike fund is obviously not a big priority with you."

"Must not have had your prunes for breakfast, eh Finnegan? Or are you worried about getting a hernia carrying that briefcase? What do you have in there, a basketball? Twenty thousand dollars?"

"What?"

"Sit down."

Castle patted the bench and Finnegan approached tentatively.

"I am working, kid. This is the old newspaper gaff."

Finnegan sat, put the briefcase on his lap, and held it with both hands.

"Why didn't you come to the meeting?"

"Just like this fellow here in the paper, Joe Frontenac, 'I was there.'"

"You most definitely were not. I specifically made it a point to look for you."

"The union has a new member, Comrade Salinsuk."

"What?" Finnegan appeared befuddled. "I don't understand what you're saying."

"You were very good, Finnegan. I especially liked the way you said, 'Order, order.'"

"You mean you came in disguise? Isn't that sneaky, spying on our comrades?"

"That's rich, Finnegan. Sneaky! It was sneaky to steal twenty thousand smackeroos too. I was in my proud Galician worker's get-up. I sometimes like to lose myself in another

41

identity."

"You don't like me much do you, Castle?"

"Oh, you're all right but I won't let any strong affection stop me from blowing the whistle on you if I find out it's you that copped the loot."

"Me! Now see here..."

"What I see is that there were only four of you who knew the combination to the safe. Am I right?"

"Yes, that's correct."

"And you don't suppose Rose Jenkins stole the money do you?"

"Certainly not. Don't be absurd."

"Well then I didn't go to McGill like you but I can still figure out that we're left with you, Harry Green and Alex Tremaine. Assuming it is an inside job which, for the time being, we, or I, must assume."

"You're not serious?"

Castle shrugged. "Who is this Alex Tremaine anyway?"

"I can assure you," Finnegan said indignantly, "that Alex is of unimpeachable character."

"Yeah, yeah. With your assurance and twenty thousand dollars in my hands, I'd have this thing wrapped up. Look at it this way, you're not snitching on anybody but by telling me something about this unimpeachable character you may lead me down another avenue, so to speak. See I may ask you a question but really be just as interested, or more interested, in what you say that seems irrelevant or superfluous as in the answer itself. Get it?"

"No."

"It is the oblique or indirect technique favoured by us really smooth operatives. But never mind. About Tremaine."

"Well, I suppose there is no harm in telling you that Alex got into some trouble because of a strike action down in North Carolina. He was organizing the textile workers against the Bedaux system down there. I suppose you know what that is, the Bedaux system? Especially since his name is all over the papers these days because of his connection with the Duke of Windsor."

"I knew about it when you were in short pants."

"Yes, you must be all of six or seven years my elder. Anyway, Alex Tremaine fought bravely against an inhumane system designed to extract that last bit of energy and dignity from the worker."

"Uh huh."

"So that is how Alex came to be in Canada, by fleeing over the border when he got into trouble."

"Where's he from?"

"The United States."

"How do you know?"

"Well where else could he be from?"

"Beats me."

"Alex was in Massachusetts years back, fighting to free Sacco and Vanzetti. Since Alex knows some Italian he was able to befriend them."

"Fine resumé, I'd say."

"Yes. He has a good many admirers. Harry Greene has been a fine soldier for the cause but plenty of us feel that he is, well, he is just too old."

"Fifty-six, if a day. So the torch is passing, eh? Or it's being grabbed."

"That's a rather crude way of putting it," Finnegan said. "There will be a fair election. Harry Greene simply has not changed with the times."

"There doesn't seem to be any motive for Tremaine making off with the loot, nor Harry Green, and we've struck Rose off the suspects list. But you don't have their kinds of credentials do you, Finnegan? Yours is a comfortable, bourgeois background. Studied law at McGill. You haven't had any money the last couple of years and you're used to having it. You must have been missing it all this time."

"Oh, balderdash."

"Ah! I'm aghast, you using that word. Please try to maintain the gentility expected from one of you background."

"Before I defend my background, which I shouldn't have to do, and solely for the sake of logic, why should you dismiss Harry Greene so readily?"

"Ah, the light shines on you, and you waste no time deflecting it, do you?"

"Not that I suspect Harry Greene, but because your reasoning is suspect, I just want to point out that an entirely objective person would quite easily detect motive. His time is past; he knows he is not going to be elected; such a circumstance could lead to bitterness."

"And to assuage his hurt feelings, as well as get even, Harry Greene steals twenty thousand dollars."

"It is reasonable. As reasonable as what you said about me."

"I'll grant your point, only I know Harry Greene and he is incapable of doing it."

"Nathan Leopold's mother probably said the same thing."

"She knows Harry too?"

"What? Oh, for Pete's sake."

"Let's get back to you. You studied law at McGill...."

"And I also worked in logging camps."

"Sure. On your summer holiday one year in the Laurentians where you could flee to your family's cottage on weekends. And you weren't a faller or even a chokerman. You were the bookkeeper. Your old man got you the job. When you got your degree, you headed west."

"How do you know all this?"

"Don't seem so surprised. I've been earning my begrudged fee."

"I worked my way out west, so I know what it's like to toil for a pittance."

"But you never *had* to work. You put in a day here, couple of days there, like a dilettante, like of one those reporters the

44

papers send down to spend a night in a flop house, like this yo-yo I mentioned before, this Frontenac. Anyway, no sooner were you in Vancouver than you took off with the On To Ottawa group but you only made it as far as Vernon. You must have ascertained that it was bound to get nasty somewhere down the line. You weren't in Regina when the cops jumped out of the van and started shooting, were you?"

"No, I was not. Were you?"

"I had a previous engagement."

"And it paid well, didn't it?"

"Not enough, especially when you figure in the three months in the calaboose. But I don't want to bore you with my reminiscences. Why don't you just tell me if there is anyone hanging around the clubhouse who looks more suspicious than the rest. I know that might take some serious ruminating. Judging from what I've heard and what I saw last night, you got the manpower there to fill any request. I mean the bulls could roust the lot of you for looking suspicious. There must be a pete man or two in the crowd but the trouble is, as you've probably learned in one of your classes at McGill, like maybe Insight into Criminal Behaviour, yeggs and pete men are generally inconspicuous fellows. So let's stick to suspicious. Well?"

"We do get a number of transients. They generally visit once or twice, and disappear. There is no way of keeping track of their movements but there is one fellow. But then again, no..."

"Come on, you've committed yourself."

"He's what I would call a religious fanatic."

"Then he must be guilty. We know what Uncle Karl and cousin Vladimir Ilyich, or whatever his real name is, think of that sort, eh Finnegan? You want I should just liquidate him? Save the WUA a lot of money?"

"I'm beginning to understand why you've only had one other customer."

"Two. But maybe you're right. Tell the truth I could have

45

had a third client. Guy owned a couple of gold properties, wanted me to pose for him as a mining engineer. Not pose for him personally, you understand, but up at his properties near McGillvray Falls; snoop around, see who's making off with fifteen percent of the payroll every month. Well you can bet your ass, I told him to get lost. I mention this merely to advertise the fact that I do have some moral sense remaining."

"I can breath easier now."

"No, you can't because you're going to worry whether or not I suspect you. Which is what I want you to do. Now about the bible thumper."

"I know nothing of his background. He calls himself the cousin of Jesus and the brother of somebody else. A woman. Let me think."

"Can't be too far gone, eh? Only Jesus's cousin. Who's the dame?"

"I can't recall. Maybe it's a former wife or girl friend who became fed up with his relentless proselytizing. Anyway, how important can it be? The point is he is always hectoring people and signing petitions and what not with a cross and his name written in the cross."

"His name?"

"Emile. He's French. Last name is, I believe, Lousieux, or something like that."

"*Lisieux?*"

"That sounds like it."

"Not up on recent hagiographic developments, are you Finnegan?"

"No, but I suppose that is one of the trivial ways you fill your idle moments."

"Ah, is that the inherent sarcasm of your elitist background rearing its protestant head? I knew you had it in you. I tell you though, Martin Finnegan, you'd do well to pattern yourself after your namesake, Martin of Tours, patron of beggars. Mine is Eugenius of Carthage who protected his flocks from van-

46

dals; kind of fits present circumstances, eh? I admit I didn't know this at the time of my sojourns in that part of the world. Interesting symmetry, I'd say. And he kept getting banished, too; which also fits. But getting back to your man. Description, please."

"Tall and thin, long black hair. He has intense eyes and never blinks. When he is not talking about his two obsessions, he is trying to borrow money."

"Certainly didn't see anybody fits those particulars last night."

"We have to ban him from general meetings. Now that I think about it, I haven't seen him for several days. Since the robbery. I know he had a room somewhere near the foot of Cambie Street, I believe it was. I could ask some of the others for more information."

"No, thanks. That's my job."

"I must tell you, Castle, that I am quite aware of my background, my elitist, as you've called it, background, but..."

"But that is an unfortunate accident of birth. Beneath all that beats the heart of a true Stakhanov."

"I cannot pretend to be a worker, and I have stopped making the attempt. I have come to know myself. I can, however, serve the revolution in other ways."

"Yeah, as a leader."

"As a lowly secretary, if need be. Or in any other way that I can be of use. I dream of a better world for everyone. What do you dream of?"

Castle looked away from him. Down on Hastings Street, an old fellow with two canes was staring up at the cenotaph. The sun shone through the trees and the little park was now all in chiraroscuro. Most of the business types had gone back to their offices. Two Indians coming down the hill, saw the sleeping Indian and went over and sat down next to him. The man woke and, after a moment of staring groggily, reached for the bottle. It was still there by his belly. He handed it to one of his friends, a heavy-set older man, who pulled the cork, tilted the bottle so that a few drops spilled onto the ground, and then had a long drink, before passing it on.

"Did you see that, Finnegan?"

"You mean the poor Indians spilling wine in their haste to find oblivion?"

"Naw, he spilled it on purpose."

"What do you mean? Why would he do that?"

"It's done as homage, a sort of benediction to all those drinkers who've gone before, who've lain down on the ground with their bottles and never gotten up."

Castle stood. "You're okay, kid. It's been nice chatting with you but I got to go. I'm working on a case."

Finnegan remained seated watching him. Castle walked up the hill, left the park, crossed Hamilton Street and when he was lost in the crowd on Pender, Finnegan rose and went the other way, down the hill.

Chapter Seven

When Aarno Kranjola was ten years old he joined his father, two brothers and a little, long-haired horse in the Finland forests to chop down trees, cut them up and haul them out. This they did all year round and sometimes in the winter, Aarno's hands would be numb from the cold but he was allowed no respite from the work. And why should he be? His father's hands were numb, his brothers' hands were numb. Aarno worried that he could no longer draw pictures if his hands stayed numb. But then, when he wasn't in the woods, he was usually too tired to draw pictures. He felt sorrier for the little horse than he did for himself. When he was fifteen years old, and six feet one inch tall, Aarno left the forests for good, or so he thought. He got on a tramp, worked his way around the world twice and jumped ship in Vancouver with the Polish first mate who convinced him there was money and a better life to be made on these shores.

Aarno immediately got a job washing dishes but it didn't pay anything so, three weeks after going on the sneak, he found himself cutting down trees a day's boat ride north of a town called Powell River.

Everything they said about Canada was true, a man could work hard and make a lot of money. Aarno was the best worker and one of the strongest men in the bush. When he was twenty-five years old, a drag chain opened up his skull.

Aarno was in his usual spot, a camp chair under the Birk's clock at the intersection of Granville and Georgia. He had his easel in front of him and a box of charcoals and pastel sticks on his lap. He was waiting for a customer. A fine artist, Aarno, but one who didn't get much business. His looks scared away potential patrons. Aarno was huge. His head was split by an inch wide furrow that ran from his crown to the bridge of his nose. He was bald except for hair which sprouted from the furrow like grass from a crack in the sidewalk.

When he saw Castle, Aarno smiled. Whatever the doctors did to him to put him back on his feet had the simultaneous effect of extracting all the violence and bad-feeling from Aarno's character. Now he had the smile of the famous, ring-letted little girl in the motion pictures. Should Aarno ever go to sea again, it would be on a good little ship called Lollipop.

"Well, Gene. Tell me, have you come here to have me draw your portrait?"

"No, sir. That would be vain of me, wouldn't it?"

"Vain? What is this vain?"

"A guy who is shallow and overproud. Like in the bible, *'Vanity, vanity, all is vanity.'*"

"I never read the good book."

"The fellow I'm trying to find reads it, and it's his picture I'm hoping you can draw."

"Yes. It is said that everybody in the city passes underneath the clock at one time or another and I haven't missed a day here in four-and-a-half years. I may not have read the good book but I thank God for letting me come to Canada

50

where a man can always be making a living even when he hurts his head."

"Aarno, this guy may be French, French Canadian; long-haired, maybe not dressed like the fellow in the Eaton's catalogue, and he keeps a cross hung around his neck."

Aarno nodded his extraordinary head.

"That is poor Emile. He used to stand right here and preach to the people. He has not been around for a week. I hope there is nothing wrong with him. You want I should draw his portrait?"

Castle said he did, and Aarno made rapid swipes on his pad with a little grey charcoal stick in his short, blunt fingers. Not exactly your sensitive artistic hands, Castle thought to himself. Aarno worked some more with a black stick, then a purple one and in two minutes handed over the result. Castle was amazed by the eyes that were alive in the gaunt lines of the face. He had seen eyes like that in pictures of Rasputin and in deer surprised in the forest, and he was amazed that anyone could reproduce just that look and feeling in so short a time with three pieces of chalk and charcoal. He thought of Aarno grabbing a stick out of the fire and telling a story on the wall of a cave.

"This bird ever mention where he lives?"

The man looked at Castle as he considered the question. His eyes were softer than hazel, almost golden. They hid nothing. "He used to say the trains were keeping him from sleep at night. That is all I know."

Aarno shrugged his massive shoulders and said he was sorry he could not be of more help. Castle said that was fine. He thanked Aarno and offered him a dollar for the portrait, but the man wouldn't take it. They wished each other well and then Castle went off down Georgia Street carrying the nine-by-twelve portrait of a religious fanatic who might have turned thief.

He took another look at the portrait while he waited on the

51

traffic light at Richards Street, and became aware that two people beside him were looking at it too. They were probably mother and daughter. When he glanced at them, the woman turned her head but the girl, she might have been fourteen, smiled.

"I don't really think it looks like me," Castle said to her."What do you think?"

She giggled. Her mother tugged at her arm and they started across the street.

Chapter Eight

High noon and old man Pattison had his nine-year-old son out front of the Pentecostal storefront church making like Gabriel to round up the sinners. The father used to be there himself sermonizing before he got a job selling used cars. The kid blew trumpet for the midday feed then hustled pumpkin seeds in the East End until the evening meal.

"Hiya, Jimmi."

The carrot-topped tyke nodded the horn without missing a note of "Bringing in the Sheaves." Only when the joint looked like being full did he stop bellowing his cheeks like a budding Bunny Berrigan and go inside.

Castle followed as far as the door, mumbling to himself, "I got a house, a showplace still I can't get no place..."

A quick survey of the flock assured him that there might be a couple of true spiritual searchers up front but the rest were strictly refugees from the street trying to keep their eyes open until the sermon and the hymns were out of the way and they could get down to tomato soup, stale bread and weak java.

A few minutes later, Castle peeked in at the Gospel Temple before calling at the Carrall Street Mission but there was no one at either place who he'd take to be Jesus' cousin, or an intimate of St. Theresa. He didn't think there would be, Theresa being on the roster of another team. But the Catholics weren't giving away any free chow in this town, and he would be remiss in not going through the motions. Also, that line of thinking might be logical, and in this business you couldn't take anything for granted Then again, you steal twenty grand you don't have to suffer for your tomato soup. Unless, that is, you're nuts.

It was curious that at three missions for the unfortunate, he'd seen no incognito newspaper reporters. Must be a big day for fires, Castle concluded.

What Aarno had said about the trains keeping the fellow awake fit with Finnegan's statement that he had a room at the foot of Cambie Street, so that's where Castle went. There were sixty feet of Cambie on the other side of Water Street before it ended at the railway yards. Just enough room for the building on the corner and a narrow three-story hotel. A sign on the door told him to see the manager in room "#1" which was up a flight of stairs—the second floor if you wanted to look at it that way.

His knock was answered by an emaciated-looking woman in a robe opened over a clean but tattered satin slip. You could see the veins in her throat and the saddle of bone that they rose out of. Her hair was limp but she had put on a little eye shadow that morning. The woman looked like a tired forty-five but was probably a tired thirty-five, and somewhere in her face was the memory of dancing all night.

"Hey, I know you from somewheres."

"Yeah. Didn't you used to work out of Alexander Street?"

"That I did. I call myself Mommy now. Come on in and meet Daddy."

Daddy was a six foot four inch welterweight who sat at a

round table in his pajama bottoms, slippers and flannel shirt with the newspapers spread in front of him and opened to the sports pages. There were two decks of cards and half a dozen glasses on the big table and in some of the glasses were traces of something alcoholic.

Daddy looked at Castle and invited him to have a seat and a drink. Or at least one of Daddy's eyes looked at him, the other was trained on something to Castle's left and behind him. Another guy, perhaps one of the knights of the card playing table, was asleep the couch. He had a potbelly and a moon face and the back of his neck rested on the bulbous arm of the couch, affording Castle a good view of his nostrils. It was like looking into the business end of a double-barrelled shotgun.

Castle thanked Daddy but said he couldn't stay long. He took the portrait, folded into fours, out of his inside jacket pocket. He had put it away because of all the art critics on the street. "Listen, maybe you can help me."

He held the picture up to Mommy, then to Daddy. "You rent a room to this guy?"

"You a cop?"

There was an east coast American accent to Daddy's voice, but no menace in it.

"Come on, Daddy, don't insult the fellow." Mommy urged. "He's a rounder. I know him from the old days."

"Okay. I'm hep. We got to be careful, pal. We have all night card games in here. Make a little book. Mommy and Daddy got to get by. Guy you want is in room one-fourteen upstairs but he's not in now."

"Does he owe you any rent money?"

"Guy may be unusual, more than unusual, but one thing about him, he always manages to make the rent. Works a couple hours a night somewhere."

"You think I could have a look at his room? I'm working on something private."

"Sure, why not. Mommy, give him the key."

She took the key from a board on the wall by the door, and looked over at her husband who was intent on his newspapers. "You want me to lead you to the room?"

When she said it, handing him the key, Castle finally realized who she was. He shook his head. "No, don't trouble yourself. I'll only be a minute."

Number one-fourteen was not the room of a slob. You could have bounced a nickel on the bed. What few clothes there were hung neatly spaced in the closet, broom and dust pan waited in a corner. A simple wooden chair was pulled up to a small wooden table on top of which was a pair of scissors and a thick candle upright on a saucer. A regular penitent's cell, thought Castle, save for a four-foot-high stack of paper bags at the side of the desk.

Castle frisked the clothes in the closet, had a peek under the pillow and the mattress, and under the bed but he didn't find twenty thousand dollars or any portion thereof. What he did find under the bed were two piles of brown paper that had been cut from bags and covered in a neat back-slanted hand.

He glanced at a few pages before replacing them, making sure the stacks were exactly as he had found them. He left the room and returned the key to Mommy.

"You know where this bird hangs out?"

"Yeah," said Daddy. "He carries this sack he probably swiped from the *Times* but what's in there are paper bags that he's always writing on. Won't let nobody see them. He looks for a place to sit, and he scribbles till someone shoos him away."

"Well thanks for your help."

"Think nothing of it."

Castle went out and Mommy followed him into the hallway.

"You got time for a drink? You know, for old time's sake?"

56

"Got work to do. You're off the stuff, eh?"

"Three years now. Daddy too. I met him and we kicked together. Just quiet booze artists now. You know, I remember, before you took up with what's her name, how we...Ah, the hell with it."

"See you around, Francie."

"Sure, Gene."

He was sitting on a crumbling concrete stairway facing the train tracks, a green fountain pen in his left hand, and he was covering one of his paperbag pages with ink. The building that had once been attached to that stairway was long gone, and what remained of the steps was almost smothered by young blackberry bushes.

Castle scuffed the gravel and kicked at the weeds but the man gave no sign that he heard. Finally, without looking up from his papers, he said, "You've been sent to get me, eh?"

"What gives you that idea?"

"You are a private detective, what they call it?"

"Who in hell told you such a thing?"

"I just *know* it."

Finally the man looked at Castle or, rather, turned his black eyes on him and the black eyes did the rest. "They sent you from Corsica, true?"

"Not true. Never been there." Well, half of that is true, Castle told himself.

"That was a long time ago, my friend."

"Got in a spot of trouble back there, did you? You know what they say, eh? A prophet without honour."

"John, 4:44. Listen, I came out of the Legion a new man. You got a smoke?"

"No. They'll receive you in Galilee, yet. Right?"

"When I finish my mission, my life's work; my book, that is."

"*Histoire d'un âme*?"

"Just one poor soul. How did you know how I call it?"

57

"Logical deduction," Castle shrugged. "Crucifix there around your neck. St. Thesesa's name on it."

"Her work remains undone. I must unite all the humble souls to show that even though they are like me, lowly as a poor Norman nun, they can organize to better their lot which is what Jesus, who in a way that is very real to me, is my first cousin, would say to them if He was here among us. I do not say my *brother* Jesus. I am closer than that. He had only half-brothers, eh? Not of his blood. He lives through me rather than the fat pigs in the church who must be tithed ten percent of your income so that they can drive the big Cadillac and make large their dioceses. These priests they are not all good men, *mon ami*, don't be a naif. Not them with the gravy dripping down the front of them while they sit in the confession booth thinking who next to invite to the golf club. And my mother she listened and had fourteen children. The people must rise and slay the priests and the money changers and the robber barons."

"Takes money to make a revolution."

"More, it takes belief in Jesus who was a working man. He worked in wood like my father in St. Hubert, a simple carver of altar pieces."

"I thought you were the brother of St. Theresa. Her old man was a watchmaker."

Emile laughed and ran his fingers through long, straight black hair. The thumb and first two fingers of his right hand— the one that didn't wield the pen—were stained dark yellow.

"So you take me for a literal minded fool, eh? I have figured it out that at the precise moment of the death of the poor little nun her soul passed into me, possessed my soul. It was eleven September, 1897. In the morning precisely at 5:36 as the sun was rising on a bright new day, the grass still wet with the dew and all things are possible to a child. We must all be as children. I shall lead the way out on that bright new day."

"It seems as if you are possessed of the sin of pride."

58

"I did not say I was as good as Jesus or that I *was* Jesus. I am humble enough to claim only to be his first cousin."

Emile laughed again and kept on laughing until Castle spoke.

"Listen, I hear you get around. I also hear that twenty thousand dollars went mising from the Workers' Union Alliance."

"I spread my message which is a message that comes not only from my heart but from what I observe of the world. As I said, I am writing the story of a soul and its times."

"In your worldly observations, I wonder if you have observed any safecrackers among your potential disciples."

"You are looking for thieves? Why not condemn the real thieves? Big property owners like the priests and the money changers and the industrialists. All of them robber barons. Have you ever heard of them getting into heaven? No, not a one despite their so-called charities. You cannot buy a seat with the angels. But even a simple thief, a safecracker, a stick-up man, can get into heaven. Was not our Lord crucified with two thieves? Do you know how crucifixion works?"

"Can't say that I do."

"One does not die from the wounds in the skin, like when they nailed His feet and His arms, and those of the two thieves, to the cross. No. The body, it sags and one has to raise oneself up to fill one's lungs with air and finally one cannot do this any longer, and one asphixiates. Think of our Lord suffering like that. He suffered for us. I suffer for Him. And that is how I shall line up my victims. Hah! So of the brothers who were thieves, one said a kind word to Jesus and our Jesus took his soul with Him into heaven. This was Dismus and he is the patron of thieves. The other one—they may have been brothers—scorned Jesus. Were they sons of the same mother or brothers of *le pegre*? It is unclear. One went to heaven, the other to you-know-where."

"That is all very interesting but not very enlightening for the

59

case at hand."

"Is it not?"

"No. If you know something then come out with it."

"But maybe I have. The Lord works in mysterious ways and works through me in mysterious ways."

Emile threw back his head and laughed. The sun glittered in his eyes like light off pieces of broken glass, and to Castle, it seemed as if the blackberry brambles ringed his head like a crown of thorns.

Chapter Nine

The city was tucked into a dense rainforest and there were trees as far as the eye could see; beyond that were more trees, north to the Yukon border and over to the Rockies to the east; all of them, by Jesus, just waiting to be cut down and turned into paper money.

But there weren't any trees in this east end of town where Castle walked now. This was, ironically, the quarter where lived the men who felled the trees and those who put them through the mill, as well as stevedores and fishermen, and your general, all-around working stiffs the ones who still had jobs and their families. What do these sorts need trees for? wondered the people who owned the land and sold the houses. They want to look at a goddamned tree, they can jolly well cast their eyes to the North Shore mountains, or ride the trolley car across town to Stanley Park. They can gripe all they want to but what other city on the continent boasts a Stanley Park? Be there a burg anywhere that provides such sylvan glades for its inhabitants? No way. Of course, Stanley Park was in another part of town. The west end and the west side, that's where those folks lived who owned the mills, the boats, the warehouses, the factories and even the trees on the hillsides. There were plenty of trees in those parts of town, of that you can be sure. In the western quarters, the streets they didn't name after themselves or after the explorers who had made it all possible, they named after trees. There was Fir, Arbutus, Willow, Yew.

Castle was on a street called Jackson where no trees were in evidence nor did May cherry blossoms bloom but there were weeds aplenty in vacant lots. Houses built of trees were close to the curb, two-and-a-half stories high with sagging staircases that didn't even have the decency to hide at the back but hung brazenly over cracked sidewalks. Coming home of an evening after a toot you could distinguish the box that contained your own flat only by your own unmistakable junk on the landing.

Castle was careful to keep to one side as he mounted the stairs to the top floor of one building in the middle of Jackson Street. His knocking was answered by a haggard woman in a faded house dress who held a year-old infant in need of a good scrubbing. A little boy, just a couple of years older, tugged at her dress with jam-covered hands. Behind her an infant wailed from its crib, an ironing board sat heaped with laundry and an unshaven man in dirty long johns squinted at the doorway from an overstuffed armchair.

"Oh, excuse me, ma'am," said Castle tipping his hat.

"We don't want any!" bellowed the man of the house from the background in a Scottish burr.

"I was expecting to find Rose Perkins here," Castle told the woman.

She looked at him as if scared to speak, and the man pushed himself up from the chair, to shuffle over. "Who the hell's that, some drummer?"

"He's wanting the old lady," said the woman to her husband, not taking her eyes from Castle.-

62

"Oh, he is, is he? What the hell you botherin a fellow for, eh? I'm on nights. I need my rest."

The underwear bagged at the crotch and hips, and a big toe stuck out of thick woollen socks.

"Sorry, bud. Rose Perkins used to live here, I believe."

"Yeah, used to. Rose the Red. But she don't no more."

"Do you know where she moved to?"

"Yeah, I do. What's it to you?"

The man stared at Castle with truculent defiance.

"I'm an old friend."

"One of her Commie friends, eh? I'd be telling you if you were the sheriff but since you ain't you can piss off."

The man turned his back on Castle and in a toes-out waddle returned to his chair. His outfit could have used a couple of weeks in the Chinese laundry, so could his body.

The little boy pulled harder at his mother's dress and the infant continued to wail.

"She's moved down to the basement."

The woman said it in hardly more than a whisper but her husband, who was just about to flop into the chair, heard and turned around, "Beatrice!"

"Thank you, ma'am," Castle tipped his hat again.

The expression on her face was not hard for him to read, it was one of utter desperation. Take me away, it pleaded. Anywhere!

"Beatrice! Get over here!"

One bright eye, magnified by a silver dollar-sized piece of glass that was rimmed with wire, peered from the crack in the doorway and above a loop of chain, like the sun suspended over a saddle between mountains. Then the crack narrowed and widened again as the chain came off and a stout woman in a black dress stared at him quizzically and silently but only for a second before her round face broke into a grin.

"Is it really you?"

"The same, Rose."

"I'm in shock, lad. Come in, come in, you good-looking son of a gun."

They embraced as Castle stepped inside. The woman leaned back, holding him at arm's length. "Let me take a look at you, it's been so long."

"How is the queen of my heart?"

"Getting old and ornery, you joker."

"What a bunch of malarkey. You've always been ornery."

"Getting worse. Breathing don't come easy these days and I got a touch of the gout now and again but I can't allow myself to be mellowing, not with so many bastards running around out there."

Not much sunlight got in through a window that provided a good view of the footwear of passersby. Yet the cluttered flat was homey. Despite a potbellied stove and a chesterfield with doillies on the arms, the room was dominated by bookshelves and a rolltop desk stacked with papers.

"Speaking of bastards, Rose. I just me the one upstairs. Called you a Red, he did."

"If I could climb those steps, I'd settle with that MacDonnell, you better believe it. Me, a Red. Humphf! The ultimate insult. But I'm forgetting my manners. Care for a mug up? Yes? Well make yourself to home while I see to it."

Castle sat at the end of the chesterfield closest to the kitchen and watched Rose pour water into a black-and-white speckled kettle.

"That lardass up there?" she said, striking a match at the two-burner gas stove. "He thinks the sixty hour week is a pinko notion."

"Yeah. Reminds me, this fellow Finnegan, Secretary of your group, I wonder if he's ever met that sort of proletarian."

"Hah! If he met MacDonnell, he wouldn't see a corpulent scissorbill but a muscular Joe Hill that's inside trying to get

64

out."

"By the way, what do you think of the kid?"

"Finnegan? Every radical organization has its Finnegan. Oh, his heart's in the right place, I suppose. For now. Trouble is when he gets disillusioned, assuming he will, it's a hard fall he'll be taking. His kind always does. Finnegan is precisely the sort who becomes a comintern hack. Number two at the censorship bureau in Minsk, kind of thing."

The tea kettle whistled.

"Be with you in a minute, Gene."

Castle scanned the bookshelves. The flat may have been different but the actual volumes were familiar. Morris and Malatesta. The complete pamphlets of Johann Most, the *Collected Jack London* and Berkman's *ABCs of Anarchism*. Whitman too, and Heine.

Rose came out of the kitchen and Castle took the tray from her, put it on a footstool in front of the chesterfield. Rose sat and sighed, took up her cup. "Speaking of disillusionment, how in hell are you, Gene?"

"You're the second one today who's brought that up."

"There might be hope for you yet."

"Thanks. You know I'm looking for the stolen money, eh?"

"Harry Greene phoned and told me. By the way, he wants to talk to you."

"Good. It's been awhile since I've seen Harry too. So tell me, who's got the moo-la?"

"You can search me." Rose said. "Anytime."

She winked and laughed, and Castle laughed with her.

"Ah, Gene. It's so good to see you. I haven't had more than a half-hearted chuckle in donkey's years. Lord knows there's not many laughs around these days. Ah, you remind me so much of the Doctor. But you know that. Cut from the same cloth, the two of you. No patience with meetings and the like, always going off on some crazy scheme. Always coming back though. Might take a month, a year or a goddamned decade but you always get back. I miss that bum."

"I miss him too. The Doc, he was kind of a hero to me when I was a kid."

"Yeah, he was my hero too."

Rose sighed deeply. "So why'd you come to see me? It ain't smooching on your mind."

"What's the line on this Tremaine?"

"Only met him a couple of times. He just appeared, oh, six months ago. On the lam or something. Not my type, mind, but he's a handsome son of a gun. Smooth operator too. He's got all the youngsters under his spell and each of the girls in a swoon. Times were different he'd make a good lounge lizard. All for starting the revolution tomorrow and, naturally, that's just what the kids want to hear. They've never had their heads busted but they probably will. They're entitled."

"He's taken his lumps, you buy his biography."

"You don't, Gene? You think he's involved somehow with the job?"

"Tell you the truth, it's not that I think he's involved in that. Why would he still be hanging around? It wouldn't make sense. There's something else bothering me. I'm not so sure what I think about his past though. Big hero from the States. With Sacco and Vanzetti, with Larry Beal in Carolina. Nothing farfetched about that, of course. Maybe it's just that I can't make the guy. What do you think?"

"I don't even know if I believed Vanzetti."

"You do me a favour? Get on the blower to some people with the textile workers? Run him down for me?"

"Sure thing. I'm in the middle of my column for *Free Thinker*. Soon as I finish that, I'll get on it. But right now, if you got a minute or two, I want to show you something."

"Sure thing."

Rose reached for a scrapbook that was on a small oilcloth covered table behind the chesterfield.

"Just got this in the mail the other day. From Doc's eldest

girl in Spokane. She found it in the attic when they were moving."

When Rose opened the book on her lap, a black puff of crumbling album paper escaped. "Look here, it's Doc and me out front of the hobo college in Chi. Most be 1911 or 12. And here he is in Centralia..."

Chapter Ten

Nine o'clock in the morning and the weather was back to normal. It was drizzling. A trolley car, two buildings on the other side of the street, and bits and pieces of several automobiles were reflected in the glass of the revolving doors. He stood holding a cardboard cup of coffee in each hand, observing the distorted tableau. At first, it reminded Castle of a fun house mirror; then it reminded him of one of those modern paintings he had seen a few months ago in Paris. Finally, with one foot, he pushed at the bottom of one of the glass doors.

He crossed the lobby and leaned with his elbows on the shelf of the dutch door. Laura, busy plugging and unplugging, didn't notice him.

"Get lost, pencil prick!"

"Ahem! I suppose that was a prospective client of mine."

"Oh, hi. No, just the morning obscene phone call. I should hire you to find out who it is."

"But you won't though because you probably don't mind

all that much."

"You're probably right. It's the only fun I get these days."

"I don't know, you could stand out in the drizzle and watch the pictures in the revolving doors like I've just been doing."

"You're a strange man, Castle. Wait a second...Yes? Beanie Brown? Who shall I say is calling? Portland Joe? Oh, no; he's not here now. Yes, I'll remind the jerk he owes you a yard. Goodbye."

"Now, what were you saying, Gene?"

"I was saying you better take this coffee so you don't have to complain about it being cold."

Laura took the top off the cup, sipped and blew on the surface. "You know, this is a pretty poor substitute for dinner and a night on the town."

"What about your gold mining executive?"

"Him? He turned out to be strictly iron pyrites. But you? There is the fabulous Louise La Tour. Which reminds me." Laura arched her eyebrows as high as they would go. "You got a visitor waiting upstairs."

"Female?"

"A *lot* of female."

"Sorry I can't stay and chat."

Laura smirked.

"Oh yeah, and Harry Green called. Wants to meet you someplace tomorrow night. Here's the message."

She took a square of paper from the spike.

"Pier Eleven at ten o'clock. Now beat it. Mustn't keep the, uh, lady waiting."

The light was on in the office next to Castle's, which meant the elusive Beanie Brown was in residence, but the prospect of an actual customer kept Castle from witnessing the unusual sight.

"Well it's about time, damn it all to hell!" was what Castle heard upon opening his own door.

SHANGHAI ALLEY

This indeed was a lot of woman. She resembled an arrangement of large balloons, immense yet curvaceous. Her yellow and black dress was a deep breath away from bursting, only the long feathered wrap seemed to hold it down. She wore a diamond necklace, a jeweled comb in her platinum hair, and a sparkling ring on every pale sausage-like finger. From one hand dangled a red sequined handbag; in the other was a corona which she raised to bee-stung lips and drew on unaffectedly.

"Hi, Skinny. I like your outfit."

"Don't you recognize it? It's a genuine replica of the curtain from the girl show I had with Wonderful Wonder Acts. Remember that?"

"Remember? Hell, Skinny, I used to watch you six times a night and matinees on Saturday."

"You could of done more than watch. You started out as a ride boy, didn't you? Well you could have taken a ride anytime you wanted."

"Would that I had known."

"Would have been the best ride of your life, bud. Still would be. Hey, you hear this race record? *Tight Like That*? That Tampa Red character, he's playing my song. But in those days, you'd just taken up with Louise, I think. And there was no hanky panky. What were you doing then? I mean with the carny, not with the girl!"

"I had been assistant to Mr. Extraordinary, the season before. You know, I'd work the crowd for the questions they wanted him to answer."

"You guys had a good gaff, I remember right. You didn't flash the cards from a hole in the top, did you?"

"No, I'd mouth them and he'd lip read. But what happened was that at the beginning of that season when I met Louise, Mr. Extraordinary was indisposed. I think he was running a wire store in Denver and got found out. Anyway he was a few weeks late and I had to do his act with Mexican Harry as my assistant. The Extraordinary had taught me lip reading

70

over the last two seasons."

"Hope you learned how to use your tongue too; you get my meaning. Ah, well. You missed your chance, kid. I only do royalty and dictators now."

"Must not get too much business around here."

"Business is fine, not that *I* work much. Not with twelve girls doing it for me."

The fat lady paused, and turned serious. "Or ten. That's why I came to see you."

"Let's go into the back."

"Sure."

"Sorry I don't have a chair to offer you."

"That's all right. No one ever does. I'll sit on the desk."

Skinny raised one buttock onto the desk—pretty gracefully, considering, thought Castle—and then the other. Her calves were shaped like tear drops, ankles incongruously slender, tiny feet encased in high heels that matched her handbag. From the latter she took another corona.

"Here, have a smoke."

Castle took it and rolled it in his fingers appreciatively.

"Damn right, it's a good one. Moreno, second in charge of all of Cuba, gave me a couple of boxes last month. As a tip. They send for me on specials."

She took a paper book of matches from the bag, folded one over, struck it, and lit Castle's cigar.

"Now down to business," she said, shaking out the match.

"Thing is, Gene. Some bastard's stolen my best girls and it's got me worried sick. It's also costing me a heap of money. Wanda? This six foot Negress? I take her out of the orphanage when she's twelve. Raise her up, teach her everything. Even prepare her to be a good homemaker, she's ever dumb enough to get out of the life and marry a square John. Dolores? English bit. Had Harry Forst send her from over the pond. Whitest skin you ever saw. So aloof she hits the high rollers in their pride. They're the ones that got what it takes to bring her

71

around, make the fire alarm go off. Silly boys. Anyway Wanda vanished a week ago; Dolores three days later. You know what that means? A thousand a week a piece, if you'll pardon the expression. I want you to find them for me. Obviously, it's worth a hell of a lot to me so just send me any bill you wish. I'll even throw in a bonus."

"Tell you what, Skinny. I can't promise anything on account of I'm working on a bit of business now that frankly's got me baffled. But I'll look around. For old time's sake, how bout it?"

"Old time's sake, my butt. It's the bonus you can't resist."

"You see through me. Forget any talk of a bill though. You want to do something in exchange, have the girls keep an ear open for word of any big heists."

"Deal. Thanks, pal. There's no one else to turn to. Now do me another favour, point me to the freight elevator. I can't handle those stairs again."

Chapter Eleven

There is the huge seahorse with its neck bent, looking down on the tenderloin parade, a dumbshow, gaudy even in a drizzle. In the big window and between letters that spell The Only Seafood Restaurant, Gene Castle can be seen rising from a stool at the double U-shaped counter. There he goes to the cash register where the man takes his money and his check, and rings up the sale. Castle speaks to him and the man rubs his chin before shaking his head slowly. Castle nods, the other one shrugs, and Castle goes to the door.

He steps out under the seahorse sign and onto the pavement. The streets are still crowded with shoppers and kids. One man is asleep in a doorway over there but nobody is so indiscreet as to be passed out across the sidewalk. It is, however, only seven thirty-five. The afternoon drunks have been hauled away and the nightime inebriates aren't that way yet. Couple of hours, the crowd will have been whittled down to the real goods and the real show will begin.

There is the sound of scratchy jazz and Castle looks up to

see a sunken-eyed man at an open second story window, a radio that looks like a cathedral balanced on the sill. In the window next door, a sign announces, "Revival Meeting Tonight." Sign's been there twenty years. Down the street, the Blue Eagle begins flapping neon wings.

A guy in brown-and-white shoes and a fedora, with a tan double-breasted suit covering most of what's in between, is leaning against a Desoto Airflow, and he removes a toothpick from his mouth and calls out. Castle looks, then walks over to him and they press the flesh. After a few seconds of palaver, the man jerks his thumb over his shoulder. Castle nods and the man nods, and Castle steps between a couple of parked cars and out into Hastings Street.

On the other side, he pushes open a green painted door between a transient hotel and a store that in better times sold plenty of caulk boots to plenty of loggers. Up a flight of stairs was another door the same colour only it bore a sign: Members Only.

Out on the street on God's own sidewalk you could buy just about anything you wished. If you had a hankering to stick it in your arm or explore it in bed, why, fella, you just paid your money and took it away. But, lo and behold, if you wanted a wee little taste of wine or spirits, you had to go ducking and dodging and haunting disreputable staircases that made you feel like the sinner you truly were in the Presbyterian eyes of this soggy burg.

On the other side of the ominous door, it was evening all day and all night. There were black leather banquette booths, and smoked mirrors. This was the Manhattan Club, and over the bar done in the new streamlined style, raised-metal letters backlit with violet, told you so. The same script Mussolini favoured, thought Castle.

A man at the table closet to the door interrupted himself by glancing at Castle. Turning back to his companions, two women in big hats who'd had more than a couple of maritinis,

he said, "So the guy wipes his mouth and says to the bartender, 'Yeah, pal. She was the best damn driver I ever saw!'"

There were two shrieks and an, "Oh, Charlie. You're *awful*!
Buy us another one, wouldja?"

Castle took a position at the black lacquered hardwood
counter, and the bartender said, "Howdy, stranger."

"Art. Whatta you know?"

A big and burly man with his hair parted in the middle,
Art looked like what he was, a retired hockey player who'd
acquired a modicum of polish. His arms bulged under the tailored jacket. He was that rare man who could wear a bow tie
without looking silly.

"Sweet Fanny Adams. Can I get you?"

"Vodka martini. Hold the vermouth."

"So where's Miss Jones these days?" Art asked, a minute
later, presenting the little, sweating, funnel-shaped glass in a
ham-fisted hand.

"Down in Seattle with the magician."

"You ought to make an honest woman of that fine lady
before someone like me steals her. I'm gonna own this join
someday. She could help me run it."

"She'll be back in a few days unless Mandrake saws her in
half and can't get her back together again. I'll advise her of
your offer, Art."

The jokester by the door guffawed loudly and both men
turned in time to see him make a grab for the waitress's rear
end. The girl was quick but not quick enough. The man managed to make contact.

Art nodded in that direction.

"First time some slob like Charlie-boy there did that to
Miss Jones, she'd dump a tray over his head; he'd sue and
win; I'd be out of business and back in Moose Jaw sharpening
skates at the rink. Now what in hell brings you in out of the
rain?"

"The rain. And the fact that I'm wondering if you heard

anything about two young ladies missing from Skinny O'Day's."

"Nope. Maybe they just quit due to finding regular employment."

"Yeah, probably, that's it. They only pulled in five yards in a slow week, and I hear a girl can make twelve whole dollars as a stenographer, she's good."

"Funny world we live in."

"Speaking of which. You seen the Ferret around?"

"No, I just came on shift though. Beanie Brown's over there in the corner behind the coat stand, maybe he knows something."

"Give me another of these and whatever the Bean's drinking. I'll go over and confer with him."

Beanie Brown's countenance resembled what a kid with his first crayon would come up with if you told him to draw the man in the moon. But the kid might not have thought to add the green eye shade. Beanie wore the visor to compensate for eyes like wet raisins.

Glancing up from his Racing Form, he reached for the rye and water as if he was expecting it.

"You're welcome, Bean."

"Yeah."

"What gives, Bean? You put in an appearance at the office today and started tongues to wagging. Oh, yeah, and you owe Portland Joe."

"That's why I was in the office, hiding out."

"Yeah, nobody'd expect to find you there."

"Had to lie doggo til the baseball results came in."

"Living on the edge, eh? Betting the customers' money."

"I'm good for it. I settled with him at the card game back of Western Gym. And what're you doin these days?"

"Chasing yeggs. So how's the action on Louis-Schmeling?"

"Heavy on Louis despite him being five to one favourite."

"I'll take some of that."

"See what I mean. I tell you, guy could retire with good money down on the Kraut."

"You kidding or what? This kid's unstoppable. What's he, seventeen and oh?"

"Uh huh. And maybe he's overconfident. And maybe he's smoking too many of them muggles. Me, I got a grand on Schmeling."

"No wonder you got to duck and dodge guys like Portland Joe."

"I got a feeling about it. He's going to deck the kid for his Fuhrer."

"You're dreaming, Bean. Listen, you see the Ferret around?"

"He was at the morning workouts, last I seen of him. Tomorrow being race day, he won't be hard to find."

"See you around. Hate to run out before you can buy me a drink?"

"So what's a drink? Take my advice and go with the Kraut, you want a gift. I'll give you one to fourteen on a knockout."

"Impossible."

"Yeah? Well I hope you pick villains better'n you do fighters."

Castle had almost made the door when Charlie-boy, the fanny groper, came out of the washroom and saw him. His suit was wrinkled, tie loosened, face flushed. He was buttoning his fly.

"Hey, hey there. If it ain't Mister Castle."

Castle nodded at the man and kept walking.

"Hold on there. What's your hurry? Come on and I'll buy you a drink."

Stepping closer, Charlie-boy said, out of the corner of his mouth, "I can fix you up with Mildred over there. The one in the hat with the grapes on it. She's got hot drawers, you know what I mean."

77

"Sorry, sport. I'm working."

"C'mon, relax. Live a little. I hear you're in the same line of work as me now. We should go into partnership. Pretty soon there wouldn't be no competition, coupla smart cookies like us."

"I'm doing all right as it is, Charlie-boy."

"Don't shit an old shitter, Castle. What you're doin probably is running down some grifter stiffed a whore out of a deuce, or maybe a goniff working the short con back of Woodward's. Ain't you tired of that penny-ante stuff? It's strictly honky tonk. I tell you what, insurance fraud is big now, factory snooping."

"I bet it was you handled the Goldbridge payroll caper up at McGillvray Falls."

"How'd you know?"

"I guessed."

"That was good but I got some better action going. Do some work for people overseas. Important people. High up in the German government. What I do, I track down some scientists, people who know too much, ship them back. They're all kikes anyway. Might only take a few hours. No more than a few days. Money's good. Damn good. Come in with me, you know what's good for you."

"No, thanks, Charlie-boy. I'll stick with the honky tonk stuff."

Castle walked away from him, and Charlie-boy watched the door close. "Yeah, and screw you too pal. You'll get yours."

The rain has stopped and there is just enough light from a street lamp up ahead, and a couple of bare bulbs over back doors, to leave a sheen on the narrow macadamed alley. Castle begins walking. There is a loading ramp ahead, trash cans tight against the walls except for the inevitable one that has overturned and spewed its refuse. A sudden rustling sound causes him to wheel about and face the loading ramp, dipping slightly as if about to sink into a crouch. He relaxes when he sees the Indian man and the Indian woman locked in an embrace. They look at him with surprise, mouths opened. The woman's blouse is undone. Castle tips his hat, averts his gaze, and continues on his way, past a parking garage and a dozen barred windows. He turns at the end of the alley and heads down the street toward the sign that means home: The Rose Hotel.

Inside the room, Castle shakes out his wet coat and drapes it over a chair, tosses his hat at the hook by the washroom door and switches on the lamp next to the metal alarm clock on the bedside table. There's a pint of rye and a glass on top of the dresser so he pours himself a conservative drink, thinks better of it, grabs the bottle and goes over to the window, sets bottle and glass on the sill. A pair of Louise's panties hang from one of the knobs at the back of the chair, and he consciously avoids paying them much attention, as he pulls the chair over to the window.

Once settled, drink in hand, Castle looks out past the rusted top of the familiar sign to the window of the hotel opposite. Two old-timers in their undershirts are seated at a table, each of them with a bottle of beer by one hand and five cards in the other. Each has his own pile of wooden matches. Castle thinks about being one of them. Thinks about how it happens in the blink of an eye. He raises his glass in a toast to the old timers, puts his feet up on the sill and leans back in the chair. Takes a sip. It was going to be a big night.

79

Chapter Twelve

The sun came out in the morning mystifying the populace and drying the rain-soaked streets. Someone swept away the garbage and uprighted the metal can, and the alley was as clean as it ever was liable to get. One could for a little while forget about the people who had to pick through the refuse and steal a little love by the loading ramp or did any number of other things in alleys at night. It was a sunny morning in May and a clean slate.

The fellow in the chair at the opening of the parking garage with his official attendant's cap pushed back on his head in acknowledgement of the fine morning, gave a little wave to Castle who arrived in search of his vehicle.

Castle walked the double line of angle-slotted cars to the very rear, his footsteps amplified in the concrete cavern. He got into his own car, a seven year old, gunmetal grey Plymouth coupe, backed and turned and drove out of the garage. The attendant waved to him again, there being so little else to do.

He drove east and parked on Renfrew across the street

from the racing grounds. This he did from habit rather than a conscious desire to avoid the traffic in the official parking lot. It was a gesture to his old man and the old days. When the old man was in town back then, long before the War, between jobs in the bush, they'd ride the street car to the end of the line and walk through what was then still woodland to the brewery. There the old man would join his cronies in the beer gardens for a couple of pints, to cut up touches and discuss the ponies. Castle had liked sitting in the midst of them, listening to the stories and the bull. To him they all seemed like tough men and the old man the toughest and the biggest. When Stumpy Williams blew the call to post, they'd rise and head for the track. Until Castle was ten, the old man would take his hand the rest of the way, and he used to wonder how anybody could grow a hand that big, each finger seemed thick as his own wrist.

Castle crossed Renfrew and there was nobody to hold his hand this time. He bought a tip sheet, paid his money at the turnstile and emerged under the covered grandstand. It was the fifth race now, and kids and a few older men picked through the stubs on the floor, looking for discarded money tickets. There was a long line of betting windows and hundreds of people stood about studying their Racing Forms, and making notations in the margins. There were the usual characters who had not only the Form, but their own portable libraries of literature dedicated to revealing the sure things. You saw these guys at tables in the cafeteria, absorbed in their analyses and computations. They frowned, they scribbled with stubs of pencils, frowned again at the result, consulted the Form once more, checked another piece of paper and cross-checked against something else. At first one might have wondered what would have been the result had they applied themselves as diligently to their school studies. But on second thought, it being 1936, assiduous academic application might have landed them just where they were: at the race track at two o'clock of a workday.

81

They were all at the track too, the down at the heel and the well-heeled, some in shiny rags and some in impeccable threads. A good number were sports and turned out accordingly. The track was a refuge for fedoras and two-toned shoes. The few women in attendance were dressed to the nines and, this being serious business that was going on around them, they attracted less attention than they thought they deserved.

Castle bought a coffee and commandeered a pillar from which to survey the crowd. The fifth race was over and a few people began drifting toward the payout windows. Street urchin types worked the crowd, hawking hot dogs, pop and newspapers. He recognized a guy who had just torn up a ticket and tossed it to the floor.

"Hey, Red!"

Upon seeing Castle, the man assumed an expression of pleasant surprise.

"Jesus, Gene. You're alive."

"Yeah, despite the amount of vodka and rye consumed yesterday, I am."

"I heard reports you'd bought it in Africa or someplace like that."

"Well, as the fellow said, those reports were grossly exaggerated."

"Good. I mean, great. Fellow wants to die among his own kind, right?"

"I suppose so. You got anything today, Red?"

"Nothing-for-five. I'm skipping the sixth, claimer for maidens. But I'm going with this Lady Jolly in the seventh. The last race what looks good is Inevitable Justice."

"Inevitable Justice. Funny name."

"Yeah, so who bets a name? She's moving down from a mile and a half and ought to have no trouble with this field."

"Thanks for the tip. Who's around today?"

"The regulars are accounted for."

"Seen the Ferret?"

"Yeah, just left him. He's over by the paddock, talking to this guy. You know, the character with the turban? They call him the Punjabi Kid? Well he's with him."

"I'm going over, see what the Ferret's got."

"Nice to see you alive, Gene."

"Thanks, Red. It's nice to be that way."

Castle went out to the paddock wondering why orange hair was always called red. Someday he'd really like to see somebody with red hair.

A number of people were arranged along a whitewashed fence looking over the horses for the next race as the grooms lead them around the circle keeping them warm. One of the rail birds was a tall, East Indian, a Sikh. He was an erect and good looking man, and almost managed to appear dignified despite his brown plaid suit with matching vest, pink shirt and brown tie. He was engaged in conversation with a man shorter of stature but longer on sartorial acumen. In made to measure white suit, powder blue sport shirt and white tie, black and white kicks, glistening black and obviously dyed hair, an ex-lightweight who'd had sense enough to get out before he took too many shots, but who'd taken a few, as witnessed by his often broken nose and the shiny look of scar tissue around his eyes: Eddie Fremont, also known as the Ferret.

This man hustled at the track but earned most of his living as a fence, an occupation he was able to pursue in exchange for the occasional tip provided to those protectors of the public order. He was not, however, the sort that 'stool pigeon' called to mind, the weaselly type, in other words. Besides denoting a fur thief, another metier of which Eddie was past master, a ferret is a polecat.

The Ferret turned as if he wondering who was thinking about him.

"Would you lookit who's here," he said in a voice both gruff and ironic. "The man of the world."

"Eddie you're vined down and looking like good."

The Ferret fingered his silk tie, "'Clothes maketh the man,''eh? Ain't that what it says in the bible?"

"Says it somewhere."

"How's the gun running business?"

"Too many buyers, no challenge anymore."

"Yeah. Say, you know the Kid? Punjabi, Castle. Castle, the Kid."

"How are you?"

"Fine, as I hope you are, Mr. Castle."

"Polite, ain't he?" said the Ferret.

"Eddie, there're a couple of things I want to talk over with you."

The little man regarded Castle apprehensively and turned to his companion. "Kid? I'll see you a little later, okay?"

The man nodded at the Ferret and told Castle he was pleased to have made his acquaintance, adding, "I would be very interested later to talk with you about the business Eddie referred to. I know some people."

With that, he walked off. The Ferret, watching after him, said, "The Kid, the way he dresses, geez. I swear to God, he had that suit made for him. And he's threatened to introduce me to his tailor."

"I don't know. With the right kripani, the outfit might look good."

"Huh?"

"Nothing. C'mon, let's you and me go up with the swells and away from the smells, have us a wee dram and some conversation."

Eddie looked from Castle to the glassed-in room on the grandstand roof. "Yeah," he said suspiciously, "All right."

They called it the Cloud Room and they weren't just being cute because sometimes a gang of nimbus would hang around waiting to cross the north shore mountains, and on such occasions one couldn't see the horses at all which was rather a jolly joke. So one had another drink and mused on how it was never like this in December at Santa Anita. One couldn't, from the Cloud Room, see the hoi polloi below even on a sunny day such as this one. The place had been designed that way, thrust virtually out over the finish line. Another glass wall provided a view of the backstretch and with the binoculars you could check on your investments. Some people brought binoculars and pretended to be observing such investments in order to impress a particular party or the party in general when it was only in their imaginations that thoroughbreds were stabled. More often than not the Zeiss was out on loan from AAA Arnie's on Hastings Street and the party being impressed was some tarted-up toots, an east end bottle blonde who wanted those Zeiss herself to get another look at what makes a stallion a stallion.

Naturally because it was possible to buy a drink of spirits in the Cloud Room, one had to be a member. Thus there was someone at the door to check credentials. This particular someone wasn't above average height but he was nearly as wide. None of him was fat. He only had one arm. The wide man smiled at Castle, told him it was good to see him, and looked disapprovingly at the Ferret.

Castle lay a hand on the man's stump in lieu of a hand-shake, "Hiya, Arch. You got a table for two?"

"He with you?" the man frowned.

"Yeah, he is."

"There's a table up front in the the far corner."

"Thanks, and would you please ask the waiter to bring over a bottle of Marsala which is what my friend here drinks, I remember right."

"Sure thing, Gene."

Arch moved away and the doorway seemed huge.

After they'd taken a few steps, the Ferret said, "The creep. How'd he lose his arm? Get it stuck in the till?"

"Nothing like that, Eddie. He left it in the Somme."

The Ferret grunted, and they went to their table. Around

them was a lot of what it took to get along in the world, some of it old, some freshly minted. A waiter in a starched white jacket set down the bottle of marsala and two glasses. The Ferret reached for the bottle, and Castle clamped on his wrist.

"You pour, you pay."

The Ferret looked indignant.

"You heard anything about a big heist?"

"I might have heard about a heist but it must be only a *small* one you're interested in, it's only worth a few drinks to learn about."

Castle pushed the folded tip sheet across the table. The Ferret took a peek and wasted no time in transferring the bills to the wallet he kept in the inside breast pocket of his linen suit. Castle poured them both a drink.

"I seem to remember I heard about a warehouse job last week by the Terminal Avenue freight yards. That what you have in mind?"

"No. What I have in mind is twenty grand from a safe."

The Ferret sipped and shook his head, "Something like that I definitely would have heard of."

"Sidney Four-Eyes in town?"

"Lammed it to Frisco."

The Ferret finished the drink.

"Eddie?"

"Yeah?"

"Never call it 'Frisco.'"

"I promise. That it?"

"You kidding?" said Castle, pouring ta couple more. "Two girls. Missing from Skinny's. Know anything about that?"

"I heard a rumour." The Ferret fiddled with his glass and tried hard to sound casual, "Something about somebody making, sort of like, a raid on Skinny."

Castle stopped the Ferret's glass midway to his mouth.

"You going to give me the details?"

The Ferret hesitated and Castle filled the time by applying

86

more pressure to the man's forearm.

"All right, already." Castle released his grip, and the Ferret finished the drink in one swallow, looked around the room.

"Some guy's running them private, what I heard. But I don't know who he is."

The drink hadn't landed yet when Castle reached across the table and transferred his grip to the knot of the Ferret's tie, pulling him forward. The Ferret might once have been a decent lightweight but his willingness for the fray was always suspect.

"I got this funny feeling you do know who he is, Eddie. And you're going to tell me or I'm going to reach down your throat and take those two drinks back."

"All right. All right, man."

Castle released his grip and the Ferret bounced back in his chair, straightened his tie, arranged his collar, smoothed the front of his jacket and had a gander to see who had been watching. About half the room. "Geez, Castle. I thought you had to maintain a sense of decorum, place like this."

He ventured a grin.

"Cut the crap."

"What I heard, I heard that Augie G's got something to do with it."

"Augie who?"

"Augie G. Augie Garmano."

"Never heard of him."

"You been away too long."

"Where's he operate?"

The Ferret grunted. "East side, west side. All over the goddamned town. He's the big mahouf now."

"Where does he keep the women?"

"You mean," the Ferret grinned, "stash the gash?"

Castle glowered.

"Hey, just a joke."

"I want jokes, I'll buy the Ritz Brothers a drink."

"What you want is a lot, pal."

"Just value for my dollar."

"Yeah, right. Okay, he's keeps girls in this place on Union Street across from Holy Trinity. You're up there with the broad, keep your head up while you're working out, you can see the cross on top of the church. The bells'll ring in the belfry, you time it right."

"I think I'll pay this Augie G. a visit tomorrow," Castle smiled. "Here have another drink."

"Yeah, thanks a lot. I'll be needing more'n a drink. You got to cover me on this, Castle."

"I will."

"You better. These dagos, you don't know what they're like."

"Yes, I do. Hey, there's the call for the last race."

Castle picked up the tip sheet, glanced at it and down to the track.

"What'd you think of this horse, Inevitable Justice?"

"Forget it. She'll be lucky to finish."

"But Red says she's moving down in class."

The Ferret snorted.

"It don't matter. That nag's on the needle. She'll probably go into a nod in the homestretch. Never bet a hype horse, you should know that."

An hour later, Castle was back in his office. He tossed his hat towards the rack, missed, and left it on the floor. After assuring himself there was nothing new on the rooftops, he poured a little drink, settled himself behind his desk and in front of volume seven. The phone rang.

"Your nickel."

"Actually, it's my seven dollars and eighty-five cents, all the calls I made for you. You can expect my invoice shortly."

"Howdy, Rose, honey bunch. What'd you discover?"

"I got some things you might find of passing interest."

"You make the call to Carolina?"

"Keep your pants on. They have all new people down in Gastonia. They weren't around during the textile troubles so no luck there. I phoned this French fellow in Chicago who's high up in the Bedaux organization."

"This fellow reliable?"

"Depends on how you look at it. He doesn't like the padrone and I think he'll move on him if he gets the goods and the guts. Some bad blood back in the old country. Anyway, he was in on everything down there. Had been dispatched to Gastonia to see what he could dig up on the opposition. He never heard of our young friend, Tremaine."

"He could have been using a *nom de guerre, n'est pas?*"

"*Mai qui.* So, naturally, I described the lad in detail. Still nothing. Then I called Cape Cod."

"La di da. Who do you know there?"

"The writer Dos Passos. You know of him?"

"Yeah, even met him once, in Lisbon. Sweet, shy little guy."

"Yeah, stutters too. But don't let all that fool you. He's nothing but guts and brains. Anyway, he was there during the whole Sacco and Vanzetti trial and later for the execution. Covered it for a magazine. He knows the whole score. Guy on the order of Tremaine means nothing to him."

"All this is very interesting, Rose."

"It doesn't make the lad a thief, though."

"Nope. Just makes him a liar."

"Come around, eh Gene?"

"How about dinner?"

"Don't wait too long, honey. I'm an old dame."

Chapter Thirteen

corridor led from the main meeting hall at the Workers' Union Alliance building, past two washrooms and a janitor's closet to an office whose walls and windows, Castle noted, were fashioned from the same cheap pine and opaque glass as in his own place. Alex Tremaine was there that evening, giving instructions to two young ladies, and Finnegan was operating a mimeograph machine.

"Pay me no mind, comrades. Proceed with the revolution."

So surprised were the girls that they got halfway through what might have been the start of the Lindy Hop before concluding there was no imminent danger. Tremaine was like the gunfighter making the split-second decision that the sudden noise was no more significant than a mouse in a corner of the livery stable. Finnegan nearly had his fingers caught in the rollers.

"It would be nice," he said, switching off the machine, "If you spent as much time working for us as you do polishing your irony."

"Irony, as you must have learned in Montreal, Mr. Finnegan, is merely an indication of superficial intelligence. In my own case, I prefer to think of it as pure sarcasm."

After a full smirking moment, Finnegan countered with suspicion. "How did you get in here, anyway?"

"I knocked half a dozen times, called out your name loud enough to wake any neighborhood shift workers and, finally, feeling kind of foolish standing out there all alone, like the guy the revolution doesn't want, I took out two trusty paper clips, unbent the things, and jimmied the lock. It takes two, you know, unless you're George Raft in the movies. I always keep a few in my pocket and recommend them highly."

Finnegan sighed and turned to his colleagues, "Alex Tremaine. And Janice and Gloria. This is Castle."

Tremaine offered his hand. It was slender, the fingers long, a hand that wasn't familiar with swinging a pickaxe, lifting crates, pushing rocks around. The back of it was covered with black hair. The man's eyes were even crueller close up than when seen from the back of the hall. He had seen eyes like that before but never on safe crackers.

"So, Mr. Castle," Tremaine said, "have you any ideas as to what happened to our strike fund?"

"Damn few."

"But, surely," Finnegan said, "You have some."

"I always have *some* ideas about *any*thing."

"Are you going to tell us about them?"

"Nope."

"But..."

"But nothing."

"You could at least tell me if you found it worth your valuable time to locate Emile Liseux."

"Emile?" Tremaine blurted it out.

"Yeah? Do you know him?"

Finnegan answered for him.

"Alex is Emile's favourite panhandling target."

"He's kind to the poor man," one of the girls, Janice, said.

"He doesn't get irritated with him like some do."

"I don't know whether or not it was worth my valuable time but I did see him and it was not uninteresting."

"Well?"

"Well I turned him upside down and shook as hard as I could but twenty thousand dollars didn't fall out of his pockets."

"Maybe he's hidden the money somewhere."

"Uh huh, and maybe he really is Jesus' first cousin."

"Are you saying he is not a suspect?"

"He's highly suspect of many things, Finnegan, but safe-cracking isn't one of them. You're going to have to come up with some better leads. Running him down took half a day, and that's half of twenty-five dollars, plus reasonable expenses which consist of a nice artist's rendition of one bona fide fanatic. Well, okay, the guy wouldn't take the money. Yeah, a real wild goose chase unless he was speaking in code and dropping me hints. I'll charge a biblical concordance to the WUA and check it against my notes."

"Excuse me, please," Alex Tremaine cut in. "This is all very interesting but I must get on with the work I am doing."

Castle watched him move over to the mimeograph machine.

"We are going ahead and calling a meeting for a vote," Tremaine said. "I personally believe the members will vote to start the general strike immediately, regardless of the missing money. If it is found, all the better, of course. If not, well, nothing can stop our march forward."

Janice and Gloria nodded their assent.

Tremaine divided the papers among the two young women. "These, Gloria, are for the East End. Janice, make sure that yours are distributed all over downtown, and don't forget the newspapers."

The two women continued to look at Tremaine, hoping he

would say something else maybe something personal but, when he didn't, they turned and marched out obediently.

"So when's the big vote?"

"Tomorrow night," answered Finnegan.

"And we shall win," Tremaine added.

"The young Turks shall assume the reigns of power, eh?"

"Yes, from those who refuse to change with the times. It is just revolutionary progress."

"Reminds me," said Castle, "I got a meeting with Harry Greene at ten tonight. I wonder whether historical inevitability will be etched into his face. Probably not. I doubt there's room for any more lines and wrinkles."

"Touching sentiments," said, Tremaine, gathering his papers. "But I must be going, there is work to be done."

"Yeah, I'm busy myself."

Castle watched Tremaine head for the door. "*A presto a piu tardi, ladro,*" he said to the man's back.

Castle told himself he had seen the slightest hitch in the man's step, that no matter how infinitesimal, there had been a pause; hadn't there? He wanted there to be but he couldn't convince himself there had been, not really.

"What was that about?"

"Nothing, Finnegan. Just thinking out loud. Boy, you see the way those dames looked at him?"

Finnegan nodded.

"Don't take it so hard. Maybe it's just looks, eh? You know what they say about a handsome man being shallow. It's been nice chatting with you but I have to go now and pay a call at a high class fancy house. See you around."

Chapter Fourteen

Here I am in the dark again, Castle told himself before a narrow rectangle of light appeared six inches above his head and an eye showed in the light, like an egg yolk in aspic. It was dark again for a moment before a door opened and he heard music and laughter, and saw high rollers having a high old time.

The way Castle figured it, the only reason the little window was a mere six inches above his head was because the doorman had bad posture. As he closed the door, he thought the fellow sneered at him but it was such a long way to the guy's face, he couldn't be sure. A negro woman in a black dress, white cap and white apron took his coat but not his hat and after he gave her a tip, she pointed out the bar which he was certain he could have found if left to his own devices.

Other men had found it, still others stood about the room with drinks in their hands or sat in upholstered chairs at small glass-topped tables. A couple of gentlemen at the tables had women with them but most of the latter were in a circle on the other side of velvet ropes. The men drank and assessed them. It reminded Castle of the paddock at the track. A piano player who looked like Fats Waller was in there with them, felt fedora hat pushed back on a conk that was highly caulked.

> Say hello to love
> Invite it in for a drink
> Lay on the hospitality
> It's always later than you think.

Castle insinuated his elbow into the crush at the bar and, drink in hand, looked over at the girls and at the blue serge back of the guy next to him who was telling another guy about his escapades upstairs. Meanwhile, a dwarf in a bellhop's uniform circulated through the room.

The girls on the other side of the ropes were each possessed of a particular erotic style. Among them was a sweater girl in tight slit skirt and stiletto heels. An innocent waif wearing a private school uniform consisting of starched white blouse, dark green blazer, short tartan skirt and knee socks; her hair in two pig tails. Another girl displayed plenty of bare leg between an even shorter, buckskin-fringed skirt and the tops of white boots with spurs; a ten gallon hat was pinned to her hair and she kept time to the music by hitting her thighs with a leather braided lariat. There was also a vampire lady and the usual doxies in the usual stages of dishabille. And Wanda and Dolores were there too.

It wasn't difficult to distinguish Skinny's former employees from the others. Wanda was the only six foot tall negress in white satin lingerie. Dolores sat apart from everyone else; she was also a considerable distance removed in looks. She was pale and cool, almost demure in a dark blue evening dress. Castle immediately thought of the word 'beautiful,' and just as quickly rejected it. Here was a word you shouldn't use too often or you'd be robbing it of its power. Bring it out only on the rarest of occasions. But with Dolores, you had to skip it and go on to something else, some word that didn't exist yet. Castle hadn't believed Skinny O'Day and what she said about the five hundred dollars. Silly boy, he told himself. And here she was now in these expensive but cheap surroundings, a thoroughbred giving rides at a carnival.

The guy with the blue serge back turned around, almost knocking over Castle's martini. "Good evening, Councilman, Miller."

"Fancy meeting you here, Castle. Break open your piggy bank?"

Average height, average weight and an average paunch; there was nothing noteworthy about his face unless it was the absence of wrinkles and creases. Mr. Nondescript in a suit that didn't look like it had really cost two hundred dollars. Miller's appearance worked to his advantage. Twelve years on city council had made him a rich man.

"Yes, I did, Councilman. But they're my own nickels and dimes, if you catch my drift."

"A low inference. But I'm in an expansive mood, Castle. How do you like the merchandise tonight? They have a couple others that can't negotiate the stairs, you're interested in that kind of thing. One's too large, the other's a double amputee. You might find it hard to believe it but the dame with no legs makes herself a bundle of loot even if she does need someone to circulate it for her. *Catch my drift?* Yeah, she's rich that half-broad, or should I say she's half-rich? We had her at a stag last month, me and some friends."

In the background, the piano player began to sing *Stardust*.

"That must have made for a charming sight. The legless lady, a bunch of land developers and their bagman. Too bad I got out of the carney, it might make a nice act for the Ten-in-One."

"You don't like me much, do you Castle?"

"*Much?*"

"Let me tell you something, bud. It's me and my kind that are the reason this city isn't in the hands of the Bolshies."

"Thanks for letting me know, I'll sleep more soundly now. But, then again, maybe I'll stay up wondering if you really believe that."

Castle left the bar and carried his drink to a table. A bell rang, a discordant note in the middle of the song, and in a box on the wall beyond the girls, up popped a flag with a number on it. The cowgirl stood and made for the girls' private stairway.

A whore in a black slip looked after her and grumbled, "Some guy's are really hard up."

A husky voice emanated from the vampire woman, "Better watch them spurs, pardner."

At the table next to Castle sat an elderly gentleman and a very young peroxide blonde in a sheath dress that matched his silvery hair.

"I believe I like number four best," the gentleman said. "The negro woman."

"Oooh, Uncle Ralph," she squeaked. "You're not going upstairs with that, are you? And leave me down here all alone with all these men?"

"Why, no, sugar. Of course not. I was thinking that we would both go upstairs with her."

"Such a thought! It makes me feel funny all over," she crossed her arms over her chest and squeezed her shoulders with her hands. What little of her bosom that was inside the dress threatened to get on the outside. "I mean, her being a coloured person."

"The weather's turning warm, my dear. You want those summer outfits, don't you?"

"Uncle Ralph, I'd do just about anything for those outfits."

The old boy smiled knowingly, took a silver fountain pen from inside his suit coat, and made a quick stroke on a piece of paper. He'd been through all this before with a lot of Sugars

97

and had bought a lot of outfits. He folded the piece of paper
and handed it to the blonde.

"Well, then, take this over to the lady."

The girl stood up and wriggled over to where an Italian
woman in black with the makings of a moustache sat at a
table before a row of buttons. The blonde handed her the slip
of paper like she was feeding a sardine to an Alsatian and
was afraid of getting nipped. The lady pressed a button, a flag
popped up, Wanda stood and strode toward the stairs like an
Amazon crossing Dahomey.

The piano player finished *Stardust*, acknowledged the
smattering of applause with a nod, took a sip from a big tum-
bler and lit a cigarette. Short, thick, beringed fingers began to
vamp a tune. "This number...."

The voice was incongruously high and sweet, and Castle
looked more attentively.

"...is certainly...appropriate to the surroundings, I'd say."

Eight bars while Castle noted that quite a few yards of
high quality grey gabardine had gone into the tailoring of that
double-breasted suit, from the chest pocket of which a yellow
silk handkerchief spilled like bougainvillea.

"It's called, *Love for Sale*."

Many of the patrons, and some of the merchandise, snick-
ered. Castle was staring at the yellow silk tie that matched the
handkerchief when he noticed, to each side of it, what
appeared top be the swellings that breasts make. Fat men
often seem to have breasts, he told himself. But these had that
definite womanly look to them. And there was that near
soprano voice. But, hell, Fats Waller himself was an ambig-
uous sort of person.

When the song was finished, Castle told himself the piano
player was a woman. That decided, he made the trip to the
Italian lady.

"*Mama, com'esta?*"

She rotated a pudgy hand, "*Mezza mezz.*"

"The dame over there in the long dress, she's the English one, right?"

"*Numero uno, la Inglesa.* You like?"

"I like."

"*La principessa ghiacciola.* She thinks she's better than the rest."

"Maybe she is."

"You wanna find out?"

"I wanna."

The lady pressed the button. "You have another drink, she gotta get ready, that one."

She looked him in the eye, and then she laughed. Like she knew something he didn't know and it struck her as funny but he wouldn't think that way. "Sit. The nano, he's gonna come for you."

Castle wondered about her. Just what he needed, the mal occhio.

He did as directed, had another drink, looked around. The piano player was doing Louis Jordan's *Bad Luck Jack*, and Castle was looking at Wanda in white satin, thinking he at least had it better than old Jack, when a voice at his shoulder said, "This way, please."

He got up and followed the dwarf. When they were away from the crowd, the man said, "I know who you are. My name's Cholly. My cousins, Jackie and Jim, speak highly of you from the old days with Amazing Acts."

"They were good men. Friends of mine."

They reached the stairs which were guarded by an Italian man with a bulge under the left side of his suit. The dwarf showed a slip of paper to the man who glowered but moved aside a few inches to let them pass. Castle went with the dwarf up the stairs and along a hallway.

"This is it!" Cholly said cheerfully before mumbling, "Be careful."

The little man scurried off and Castle looked after him. A

door at the end of the hall was half-opened and he could see the back of a guy in there mopping the floor. Castle wondered whether he was the janitor or just a customer with an unusual predilection.

She was waiting, seated on a straight-back chair facing the doorway.

"Hello, sport. I'm Dolores."

She lost nothing being observed close up.

"So you're the English woman I've heard about."

She didn't appear overjoyed to have a client.

"I am English."

"Well I'm certainly glad to make your acquaintance."

It was almost eerie, Castle thought, the way she fastened her gaze on his. Then without moving her head, her eyes darted to her left and back again. Over her left shoulder, across the room, was a screen and a table.

He looked back again.

"Well shall we talk..."

She answered with a frown, and he looked at the table again. There was a pitcher on it, a wash basin and an ashtray. In the ashtray was a cigar butt.

"Dolores, sorry, but I think I just changed my mind." He began walking slowly backwards. "No offence but girls that chew the ends of fat cigars and leave them around all wet and soggy, never did make me feel all that romantic."

Castle's last step backed him into the barrel of a revolver.

The glance that he ventured over his shoulder was cut short by the end of the barrel jabbing at his spine. But he had seen a pork pie hat on a hatchet face that probably needed shaving every two hours. With that complexion and those whiskers, Castle couldn't help but think of ants in Ovaltine.

If porkpie didn't look very friendly, neither did his companion, the fifty-six long who had been guarding the front door. He also looked like one of those figures in the drawings in school books. There were usually five of them; the first was

100

always covered with hair and moving on all fours; the fifth resembled Finnegan. This individual here looked like number two, sort of bent over and wielding a mastadon's tibia, and in a couple of thousand years might be standing almost upright.

Mirthless laughter came from behind the screen. A man stepped out, pulling a chair after him. He picked the cigar out of the ashtray, lighted it and sat down. He had a face the colour and texture of cement, and just about as forgiving. His jaws were like steamshovels.

"And take off your hat when you're in the presence of the boss."

The order came from the caveman but before Castle could obey, he knocked the hat off with a swat of a paw like a grizzly's. Castle made as if to turn around and do something about it but the smaller man put the business end of the revolver under his nose.

The big man uttered a series of muttering, guttural sounds that sounded like "Uhh Urr Uhh. Grrr Urrr Hummmm."

Him and his buddies might have talked like that of a long-ago evening around a fire after slaying and devouring a litter of saber tooth tiger cubs.

"Put the gun away, Vince," said the boss. "And lock the door."

His eyes were the colour of cold dishwater. He showed a lot of cuff and the diamonds glittered, his nails were polished.

"Step closer, gumshoe."

The big one gave him a knee in the small of the back, and Castle stumbled forward.

"If you're the zoo keeper around here," Castle said, jerking his thumb over his shoulder, "why don't you get the gorilla back in his cage?"

Not pleased with being called a gorilla, the man grabbed Castle by the collar, spun him around and plowed his other fist into Castle's stomach. Castle sat down heavily, gasping for air.

101

"You got something else smart you wanna say?"

Castle held up one finger. "Wait...yeah...Where... where were you during evolution?"

The man looked at him thinking it probably wasn't a good thing what the gumshoe said but he wasn't sure how bad it was. He didn't know what to do. "Did he insult me bad, boss?"

"I'll tell you later, Marco."

The boss turned to Castle, "As for you. Why you snooping around here?"

"Snooping? I thought it was called something else, man goes to a cathouse."

"Yeah, you're going to get screwed all right, only not the way you think, you keep giving me lip."

"Golly, by all three of you fellows?"

The boss's face went blank except for the cold, mean eyes. He made a gesture with one hand like he was tossing bread crumbs to pigeons. The two goons lifted Castle off the floor and the boss rose wearily to his feet. He slipped a hand into the pocket of his trousers and when he pulled it out, his manicured fingers were inside a pair of brass knuckles. The punch came from his hip in a short, economical arc and blood spurted from Castle's mouth.

He put the dusters away, tugged almost primly at his trousers and sat back down.

"Now let's start over. Take it nice and easy. You know who I am?"

"Yeah, you must be the head dago around here."

The hoods grabbed Castle again but released him after another weary gesture from their boss.

"That's right." His lips parted showing some gold amongst the travertine. "That's right, the head dago. I'm Augie Garmano."

"If my lip wasn't split I've give you the first four to Beethoven's fifth."

"You think you're a real wise guy, don't you, bud? What're you making, a double sawbuck a day?"

"No. Twenty-five and expenses."

"Oh, pardon me for underestimating you. Seeing as how you're such a big shot, I'll give you another chance to be reasonable. What are you doing around here?"

"Tell you the truth, Mr. Garmano. I have simply come around to see if Dolores was here and to make sure she was well."

Garmano got up and stood behind the girl's chair.

"Dolores?"

He put a hand down the front of her dress, took hold of a breast and made like he was kneading dough. "You mean this whore?"

"I'm referring to the lady whose dress you got your hand inside of."

"But, what about...uh, yeah, the girl here. So who hired you?"

"I cannot reveal the name of my client."

Garmano nodded at his men, and they promptly shoved Castle against the wall. The boss removed his hand from Dolores breast and went into his pocket.

"Yes, I can," Castle said. "It's Dolores' family in England. Ever since her letters stopped, the family's been worried."

"That's touching."

"I knew you'd think so."

"How'd they find a bum like you?"

"The letters came to Skinny O'Day's place. Skinny opened them and referred the matter to me."

"Skinny think she's going to try and get the broad back?"

"Hell, no. It's good riddance, far as Skinny's concerned. She just sent me the letter with a retainer and said, 'Look into this. I don't want to be bothered with this shit.' You know how Skinny talks."

"Yeah, I how how she talks. So you gonna write the

broad's mother a letter, right? Tell her her daughter's doing fine?"

"Sure, that's what I'm going to do, first thing I get back to the office. In fact, I'll tell the dame Dolores is a private secretary for a big business tycoon."

Garmano grunted and his men grunted.

Dolores just stared at Castle dispassionately.

"So your job's done, gumshoe. You earned your twenty-five dollars. If you was lucky and earned that every day, you'd be just scraping by, right? Enough to pay the rent and put gas in your rattletrap."

"How'd you know I drive a rattletrap?"

"I looked at you, is how. I mean, you ain't exactly Cadillac. More a seven-year old Nash, kind of guy."

"Plymouth."

"What I'm saying, you got to have something else going on. What else you got?"

"Nothing much. A lady thinks her husband's making time with his secretary. She's right."

"I'm talking angles. You got any angles?"

"I'd get a paper route if I could but things are tough. There's a Depression going on."

"There is? I ain't noticed. Well, gumshoe, I guess that's all. For now."

"Thank you."

"Uh, boss?" It was Marco. "This guy, remember? Did he insult me, what he said about the revolution?"

"Yeah, Marco. He did insult you."

Marco grabbed Castle by the neck, shoved him back against the door and again let him have the heavy fist in the stomach. As Castle doubled over, Marco clubbed him on the back of the neck. Castle greeted the floor with his face. Marco was about to kick him in the ribs with a size seventeen when the boss called him off.

"That's enough, Marco. It wasn't that bad an insult."

104

"Oh," said Marco, stopping short with his foot. "Only a little insult."

"Yeah. Help the man to his feet and show him out."

Marco grabbed Castle by the lapels and lifted him.

"I can find my own way out, thank you very much."

Castle stumbled toward the door.

"Hey, gumshoe. You must be punchy or something. You're going the wrong way. Give him a hand, boys."

Vince and Marco ran Castle to the open window. Below him Castle saw a steeply sloping tin roof and across the street the belfry of St. Timothy's

"You got to take the back exit, guy like you. A cheap gumshoe with a split lip. We don't want the nice people downstairs to see you, the way you look."

Vince and Marco hoisted Castle and shoved him, head first, out the window. He hit the tin roof on his elbows and started the wild roll down.

There was a head like a guy with too many brains and a pointy chin, eyes bulging from folds of skin, pointed ears, and a tongue like a snake's sticking out at him, mocking him. The gargoyle smiled and Castle made a frantic, awkward lunge at it. A fat, horned paw socked him in the stomach but held him there. Castle took deep breaths and felt his heart booming in his chest, the blood throbbing in his temple. When he dared look up, the stone tongue seemed to flicker. He would have sworn it had. Hey, the thing was all right. You'd get used to it, and pretty soon you wouldn't even notice the ears. You could even have it over the house but mustn't let it climb up on the furniture.

Castle hazarded a glance back from whence he'd just come. The window had been closed and on the other side of it was a pyramid of three unsmiling faces. Garmano and Vince, and Marco's vast mug above and between them. The church bells began to ring.

"Well, good buddy," said Castle, "there's plenty around

here a lot uglier than you. See you around."

He took hold of a paw with both hands and swung out until his body was hanging over the edge of the roof. He took a deep breath and let go, dropping two stories to the ground, hitting with his feet and going into a roll.

The church bells were ringing the hour. The grass tickled his nose. He had to get up. He was afraid to feel what might be broken. He picked up the count: six...seven...

Ah, it was pretty damned comfortable right there. Eight...nine...

Ten o'clock. He was late for his meet with Harry Greene. Didn't make the bell. Eleven...twelve...thirteen. I don't think the legs are broken. Nor the ankles. Fourteen...fifteen. Wait for me, Harry. We have lot to talk about.

Seventeen.

There I'm up. Just like Tunney.

Forty feet above him there was a big man who looked about to cry.

"Ah, hell, boss. The guy got up. What'd we do now?"

"Don't worry about him, Marco," Augie Garmano said. "Vince tossed his distributor cap or he better have."

"I did, boss. I did." The hatchet face nodded like it was chopping wood.

"The car ready?"

"Yeah, boss. Waiting in the alley."

"Then let's scram."

Castle hit the button a second time and again there was only the click of the starter motor. He took his finger off the button and for a moment pretended the steering wheel was the pillow on his bed at the Rose Hotel. Sighing he reached for the door handle.

A large four-door sedan swung out of the alley in back of the mansion with its tires squealing. It was halfway down the block before the headlights came on.

Chapter Fifteen

A streetlamp threw down a patch of light, and nearby a blue anchor glowed faintly. But it was pitch black where Harry Greene stood, at the foot of pier eleven, smoking a cigarette, one hundred yards away from the tavern.

He struck a match, cradled it in his right hand and held it over his watch. Gene Castle was twelve minutes late. He saw a big tom over there having a rub against the butt end of a log piling at the corner of the wharf. Probably had a couple of girl friends waiting by the canning plant. Castle was not the kind of guy who kept you waiting.

Harry Green heard the sound that metal makes scraping along a roadway, and coming along the street were Johnny and May. They moved within the pool of lamplight, and to Harry it was as if they were on stage. May pulling her wagon heaped with sheet tin and plumbing pipe, Johnny with a sack over his back, caught there in the spot. Harry half expected them to stop on their marks, turn and begin a two-hander. They were both pushing eighty from the other side. Johnny used to be a tough old Wobbly soldier. Bosses bring in the goons, the IWW sent Johnny and a few others like T-Bone Taylor——whatever happened to him?——up against them. Johnny'd been a big, rawboned hombre, iron in his fists. Never got angry or even raised his voice at any other time. Took his lumps, old Johnny did. He heard the sound of an automobile engine and the engine being shut off. A minute later came footsteps along the wooden pier.

"Harry?"

"Gene?" he answered tentatively. It didn't really sound like Gene but he hadn't heard Gene in a few years, and, anyway, who else could it be?

But, no, something was wrong. He turned toward the voice. It wasn't Gene. Dark as it was he could make out the guy's beak of a nose, his hat with a flat crown. There was a gun in his hand. He thought about the gun. It really was a gun. The flash of light was the last thing Harry ever saw.

There were three gunshots.

Across the street, the scraping of the wagon stopped, and Johnny and May stood looking toward the pier.

"Come on, dear," said Johnny. "Let's get out of this light quick."

The gunman was a shadow moving across the walls and back to the car. Johnny used one hand to help his bad leg along, and watched as the killer got in the passenger's side of the front seat of the big car.

"May, we have to hurry."

"I'm coming as fast as I can."

They turned into Shanghai Alley. Above a short flight of wooden steps was a sign with large Chinese characters and below these, crudely draw letters: ROOMS.

"This wagon's heavy."

"Forget the wagon, May."

The car pulled into Shanghai Alley and the lights caught Johnny on the rooming house steps, May almost there.

"Lookit them, boss," said the big guy wedged in behind the steering wheel of the big car. "They must of seen us, the way they're acting. You want I should dump them?"

"No, Marco. Pull up. I know the old bastard."

"You do?"

"Stop the goddamned car."

When the boss had gotten out, Marco said to Vince, "The pardrone, he sure knows all kinds of people, huh?"

Johnny was reaching down for May's extended hand when a third hand intruded, grabbing the old lady's arm.

"Hiya, Johnny boy. Know who I am?"

"Yeah, I know who you are."

"Leave go my arm!" the old lady squawked.

"How long's it been, big John? Thirty years?"

"Thirty-three."

"Yeah, I guess that's right. I know you ain't a rat, big John. You didn't see one single thing unusual tonight."

"All I see is shit."

"Still tough as nails. But, tell me, you ever get sentimental, big John? You ever think of me?"

"Yeah, almost every night, I think of you."

"It's nice to be remembered. But, you see, big John, almost every night, that ain't good enough. So here's a little something else to make sure you don't skip no nights."

Garmano had merely to dip his right shoulder to knock the old lady down across the little red wagon. He pulled her arm toward him and brought his knee down against her elbow. The bone broke with the sound that a dry twig would make being snapped, and the old lady's cry was bird-like and brittle.

The old man, his face contorted with anger, came down the stairs after the boss, who laughed at him and yanked him forward. Johnny landed on the sidewalk on the seat of his pants, next to his woman.

"Take care of the old hag, Johnny. And keep your nose out of trouble, you know what's good for you."

"You ought to kill us, Pushy."

"'Pushy'? It's been a long time since I heard that. Nope, I ain't gonna kill you. I'm gonna let you live. For old time's sake."

The boss turned away.

Johnny, breathing hard, pulled May off the wagon and cradled her in his arms. She sobbed softly, and he stared after the sedan as it drove away.

Vince in the passenger's seat asked a question: "Why didn't you dump them boss?"

"Ah, I leave that stuff to you guys. I don't like killing so much."

"You don't?"

"No," the boss said. "I like hurting more."

The lips spread in the pock-marked face, the capped teeth glittered out of the dark, and the boss threw his head back against the seat, laughing this time like he did mean it.

Marco waited until his boss was done before speaking.

"With all respect, padrone. I got this feeling, kind of, that maybe we're making a mistake. Hurting them instead of killing them."

"Shut up and drive the fucking car."

They heard the sirens as they turned out of Shanghai Alley.

"Hey, Bud. Looks like there's something going on down there at Pier Eleven."

The headlights of the cab shone on a tight knot of people, and some of them were cops. Others were photographers, police and press, who aimed their cameras at something on the ground, and bulbs flashed.

Off beyond the perimeter of the crowd, in the shadows, were a few nighttime ne'er do wells, and some Chinese people,

111

watching silently.

The taxi pulled as close as it could get until a guy in uniform stepped in front of the hood and held up a hand. Castle jumped out, slammed the door and shoved some money through the open window to the driver. He pushed his way through the crowd, stopping short when he recognized the man on the ground.

Four cops were staring at him when he looked up. Two were constables in uniform, one was Koronicki and the other was his new partner, the gum chewer.

"You know this man, Castle?"

Koronicki was tired and thirty pounds overweight.

"Yeah,"said Castle, who at that moment figured he was considerably more weary than Koronicki.

"It's Harry Greene, isn't it?"

"Yeah, it was."

A uniformed cop told the crowd to keep back. Koronicki's partner said, "You know, you don't look so good, fella. You got a fat lip with dried blood around it and a cut eyebrow that's still wet. Your hair's all messed up and you were limping when you got out of the cab. Not only that, a cool night like this, you ain't wearing a coat."

"Very observant. So arrest me for breaking the coat law."

"Don't get smart with me, fella. You're in bad enough shape as it is."

Castle looked him over. A black-haired, black-browed, black-eyed Irishman, mean all the way through. The guy gave him the tough look—did he practice?—his mouth opening and closing on a wad of gum. Castle wondered how much time he'd have to do for throwing him off the Pier.

"I asked you a question!" The detective barked.

"No, you didn't. You just offered a summary of my appearance and warned me not to get smart with you because you're real big and strong and tough, at least that's what you tell the fella in the mirror."

112

"You smartass bastard," Walsh spat, stepping toward him. Castle thinking to himself: three to seven; be out in two with good behaviour; it might be worth it.

Koronicki stopped Walsh with his forearm.

"It is true, Gene. I mean, Castle, that you don't look so good. Why don't you tell us how come you got to looking that way."

"Simple. I fell."

"And later you just happened to be taking a taxi ride by Pier Eleven, eh?"

"It's not so unusual I'd be in this neighborhood, having an office nearby, as I do."

"Uh huh. Well I suppose we got to take you over to our neighborhood and ask you a few questions."

There was nothing on the walls but a big clock, and it was half-past midnight. Koronicki was at a wooden desk in his shirt sleeves, a cigarette stuck in his mouth. Ashes dribbled down onto a tie that was stained from coffee with cream and onto the front of a shirt that had once been white, and he didn't bother to brush them away. Koronicki was studying some papers, and Walsh, at the other desk, was looking at Koronicki, waiting. The older man glanced at the clock and nodded to Walsh who sprang from his chair and hurried to the door under the clock.

Castle was on the other side of the door in a small, windowless room, sitting on one of three wooden chairs. There was also a desk but it was pushed up against a wall and was for sitting on, not sitting at. A bare sixty watt light bulb dangled from the ceiling on a frayed cord above Castle's head, and he had just reached up and, with one finger, sent it swinging when Walsh opened the door. The detective leered at him for a moment, chewing his gum in that annoying way he had, with his mouth open, lips covering his teeth. "Let's go!"

113

Castle got to his feet, ducked under the path of the returning bulb and walked past Walsh.

"Sit over there," the detective said, jerking a thumb at a chair by Koronicki's desk.

"You told us a little fib, Castle. You said you have an office in the neighborhood but the fact is you had a meet with the deceased."

"I don't tell fibs, Inspector. I do have an office in the neighborhood, at the other end of Shanghai Alley, around the corner and across the street. I also had a meet with the deceased only I was late."

"Ah, hell, Gene. I know where you work out of and where you live and that you were supposed to meet Harry Greene and all those kinds of pertinents, but your appearance is kind of raggedy and I would be remiss in my duties not to wonder about that."

"Certainly you would but I already told you lads that I had a nasty fall."

"No were just walking along and you fell down?" Koronicki asked. "Sort of like the late-unlamented Harry the Hype probably did a lot of times?"

"No, as a matter of fact, I fell off a roof."

"Was you sneaking in or sneaking out?" Walsh said, grinning, pleased with himself.

"I was on my way out but I wasn't exactly sneaking."

"You get the goods?" Walsh glanced to see that the Inspector had heard but the Inspector was staring blankly at Castle.

"I got the goods, so to speak."

"And what was you doing in this place you fell off the roof of?" Koronicki asked.

"I was hoping to confer with this dame but she already had company and the company demonstrated to me how they didn't want me around."

"That's really interesting," Walsh said. "I got a theory that's interesting also. Want to hear it?"

"Oh, very much. Yes, indeed."

"Good. You had a meeting with Harry Greene at ten o'clock all right, and you were right on time. You talked about all this Commie crap you're involved in. Harry wanted you back in the little group on his side on account of he thought he was losing his power. You told him nothing doing, and dumped on the whole thing: the group, the bolsheviks and all that. He took it personally and the two of you went at it. You underestimated the guy because of his age. But he used to be a boxing champ back in his Navy days, and he worked you over pretty good. The only way you had to keep from getting messed up even more was to pull your piece. You did. You plugged him. Then you took off. Waited fifteen minutes, hailed a hack and returned to Pier Eleven and did your innocent act for us. You like it?"

"Naw, I don't like it because it shows an acute lack of deductive reasoning. Where did I hide out? Behind some garbage cans? Also Koronicki must know I got out of a cab and he, at least, is smart enough to have gotten the number, and the cabbie would tell you where he picked me up. There're too many holes in it."

Castle turned to Koronicki, and added, "You know, if the police department offered higher salaries to beginners, it might attract a loftier element."

Walsh glowered at him, "You're going to get yours, punk."

"Maybe so but not from you. Thing is, I think you actually might even believe in that theory. But Koronicki here doesn't."

"What'd you mean?" Walsh said, looking from Castle to his boss, who merely sighed, exhaling through his nose.

"Because you guys already made a collar," Castle said.

"We have?" Walsh stopped chewing his gum. Koronicki remained expressionless while asking a question.

"What makes you think we made a collar?"

"Because you got me out here, putting me through the motions, letting this guy work out. You thought I'd done it,

115

Walsh here and somebody else like him would be visiting me in the little room with the locked door. In fact, Walsh probably thinks he's still going to get the chance to show me the little trick with the rolled up weekend newspaper. The one they teach at the Academy. Why don't you clue him in?"

"You may be too smart for your own good, pal." Walsh told him.

Castle ignored him, looking at Koronicki. "I'm not that smart. I can't figure how you brought somebody else in so quickly. Come on, Inspector, who d'you have?"

"Read tomorrow's newspaper."

"Huh?" Walsh grunted with surprise. "We did arrest somebody else? Where's he at, Chief?"

"That'll be all, Mr. Castle," Koronicki said. His words of dismissal came out like the footsteps of a bone-weary man at the end of a long race, trudging across the finish line. "You may go now. If we need you again, we will be in touch."

Castle got up and walked out of the room, passing under the big clock. Walsh looked after him with undisguised hostility, before turning to his superior.

"What the hell was that all about?"

Koronicki bent his head to his papers and didn't offer a reply. He tapped a pencil on the desk top and cigarette ash drifted down onto the tie with the coffee stains.

Chapter Sixteen

"**E**xtree! Extree early morning edition! Waterfront Slaying...Labour Leader Gunned Down...Cops Nab Radical Rival..."

A citizen on his way to work took a paper from the humpbacked Indian who resumed his cry: "Extree! Read It Here...Waterfront..."

"Oh, hey, Gene. You got your name in the rag this morning."

He folded one and handed it over, taking in Castle's split lip and swollen eye. "Bulls do that to you?"

"No, I fell off a roof."

"Sure, sure. Extree!"

"Who'd they piEck up?" Castle asked, unfolding the paper.

"Fella by the name of Tremaine. Know him?"

"Yeah. Yeah I do."

Castle walked toward Ramona's, reading as he walked. Before pushing the door, he noticed, across the street, another guy with newspaper, leaning against a building at the entrance to Shanghai Alley. It was Garmano's hatchet-face boy, Vince.

Tommy Chew was working out at the grille like a conductor at the symphony. Maude at that moment was sliding four plates off her arms and onto a table. To the millionaire short order cook, she hollered, "Two on a raft; float em."

Somebody called Castle's name. It was Frank at a booth in the back.

"You see this thing Frontenac wrote? Some story."

Maude had a coffee on the table before he could sit down.

"Poor baby,"she cooed. "Bulls worked you over real bad, eh?"

"Naw, sweetheart. I fell off a roof."

"Sure you did, honey."

When she'd hustled off, Castle said to Frank, "This story has the guy convicted almost."

"They figure the kid shot him on account of the election coming up. They had another one of their arguments and Tremaine went after him. The guy had a real cold look to him, you know? This reporter, this Frontenac, don't say it but Tremaine must of known you was meeting Harry on the docks. You think he did?"

"Yeah. He would have heard me tell Finnegan."

"You think Tremaine tried to set you up for the fall?"

"Who else knew you were meeting Harry Greene besides Finnegan?"

"Two girls, Janet and Gloria. And whoever Harry told. Yeah, and Laura, the switchboard woman."

"So I wonder what's going to happen at the WUA. There's an emergency meeting called for later today."

While Frank was talking, old Johnny had come into the cafe. Castle saw Tommy Chew give him something in a paper bag and Johnny turn away from the cash register.

"Gotta go. See you later, Frank."

"You ain't even touched your coffee!"

Castle stepped quickly over to the old man.

118

"Johnny. Where's May?"

"I got this soup here for May. She's sick."

"I'm sorry to hear that, Johnny."

Castle opened the door for him.

"Don't go out there with me, Gene."

Johnny looked across the street, and Castle followed his look.

"Yeah, he's...wait, Johnny, you mean he's watching you?"

The old man nodded.

"I thought he was on me. What gives? How are you mixed up in this?"

"I can't say nothing about it, Gene. I'm sorry."

Johnny left the restaurant and crossed Pender to Shanghai Alley. The hood lowered his newspaper to follow the old man's progress but when he realized how long it was liable to take, he went back to reading. Johnny moved among the Chinese people like he was wearing leg irons. Vince folded the paper under his arm, stuck his thumbs in his belt loops and watched Johnny negotiate the stairs of the rooming house.

There was another old man in the hallway of the rooming house, a Chinese man with thin strands of white hair and white chin whiskers. He sat outside his opened door in pajamas with horses on them and puffed on a corn cob pipe. There was a boarded up fireplace in the room with candles and dried flowers on the mantle, and above these were photographs of different people. It was like an altar. A young girl with a feather duster approached the fireplace.

Johnny held the bag with the soup in one hand and fumbled in his pocket for his room key. May's wagon, still loaded with junk, was on the other side of the hall in front of a small door under the staircase.

The room was crammed full of things other people had discarded. By the door was a table holding piles of newspapers, magazines, pots, bowls, kitchen utensils. The table only had one of its original legs, and that hung down uselessly, the top

119

being supported by three wooden crates. Next to it set on bricks was a small dresser that held a two-burner hot plate. A cracked oval mirror was contained by a carved wooden frame with substantial bits of curlicue missing. Cans and jars, and joints of metal pipe rested on the sill of a dirty window. Shelves on the walls held ashtrays, doorknobs, an inkstand, a pipe wrench and china figurines too, none of them intact, each an amputee. On an iron framed bed in the midst of all this rested May, her arm in a homemade splint.

"Oh, Johnny," she murmured, opening her eyes.

"I brung you some soup, May."

He sat beside the bed on a paint-splattered stool and put the soup on the wooden crate that served as a night table. Johnny's banjo leaned against the wall between the crate and the bed. A hubcap, upturned on the crate, held a mound of cigarette butts. Johnny gently lifted May's head from the pillow and put a spoonful of soup to her lips.

"Swallow this now."

Pinned and taped to the wall behind May's head were photographs, and pictures torn from magazines. One of the photographs showed a woman and a child standing in front of a fence of posts and wire. There was a photograph of a child on a pony and another of a big, strapping young man shouldering an axe, one booted foot on a tree stump.

May turned her head away from the spoon.

"No more, Johnny."

"But you need to keep up your strength, May."

"For what?"

"To get better."

"I ain't going to get better."

"Ah! Does your arm hurt real bad?"

"It ain't that my arm's real bad. It's my time has come."

"Now, don't be saying things like that."

"You know what I been doing while you been gone?"

"You been up dancing?"

120

She smiled her cracked tooth smile.

"Even better. I been dreaming. I been dreaming of the ranch. Remember we lived on that ranch up near Soda Creek?"

"Sure, I remember."

"And you broke horses? And when you came back from wrangling, you took me to town and we spent all that money? I must have worn that blue dress you bought me, the one with the yellow flowers, til the new century come around."

"Those were good days."

"But then they strung you up to that bridge and they weren't so good no more, the days. That was when you went out with the Wobblies, and they cut you down and that man pushed you. Does your hip still hurt, Johnny?"

"All the time, May. All day long, all night."

"You didn't break no more horses after that."

"I sure did not."

"I had another dream that wasn't so good. I dreamed I saw that awful man last night. The one with the little holes all over his face. Isn't that a peculiar thing? Just after the nice dream, I had to go and dream that. I think I'm going to close my eyes now."

"Yes, go to sleep, May."

"I will. Maybe I'll see again the ranch and the hill in back of the bunkhouse with the blue and yellow flowers that matched the dress you bought me. Goodnight, Johnny."

"Goodnight, May."

When he had gotten his banjo that leaned against the wall, May closed her eyes. Johnny put it on his knee and began in his gravelly voice to sing:

Beau-ti-ful dream-er
love of my life....

Chapter Seventeen

The big new building stood alone on the hill like it had thrust straight up out of the ground. Cars still slowed on broad Twelfth Avenue and people poked their heads out of windows and wowed and goshed about how high it reached. Why from the sidewalk or the expanse of lawn around the building, it was like you were directly on a level with the tops of the mountains way on the other side of the inlet. On good days the mountains stood out so clearly, like cutouts against a blue sky. But today it was as if there were no mountains at all. If you met some Saskatchewan farm boy just alighted from a freight train and told him there were mountains just over there, he'd take you for that city slicker the home folks warned him about.

There may not have been mountains today but there were plenty of people, a great mob of men and women in front of City Hall carrying signs and raising their fists in the air. And there were many others hollering things at them. There were cops in the background, some of them on horseback who appeared tense and waiting.

"Unions Are Our Right...Free Tremaine...Protect Workers' Rights."

Fred from New Westminister—he refused to drop that second i—slowed the sedan, read the signs and said to Irma, "The last stone is hardly in place—why I bet the paint in McGeer's office is barely dry—and already they're out front, these agents of the Bolsheviks, stirring up trouble."

Irma nodded her head in agreement, then shook it and went "Tssk, Tssk, Tssk."

And Fred tromped on the gas pedal wishing there was an agitator he could run down.

Martin Finnegan in mismatched suit jacket and pants, steel wool hair and wire rim glasses, was standing on a jerry-rigged platform at the south entrance to City Hall, exhorting the crowd to demand their rights. Under other circumstances, Finnegan couldn't have swayed them with dynamic oratory or won them with his long history of unimpeachable radical dedication, but it didn't matter because he was in the right place at the right time, and they punctuated every phrase with shouts and cheers.

"Therefore, comrades, we can surely come to no other conclusion but that the arrest of Alex Tremaine is a bold injustice undertaken specifically to break the will of the Workers' Union Alliance, to destroy the growing solidarity of proletariate and unemployed in this city. Furthermore, as proof that the bosses and their handmaidens will stop at nothing to rescind our basic human rights—as if any more proof were needed—we have the body of Harry Greene, now a martyr for the rights of working people everywhere. It is time..."

Saved by martyrdom from the scrap heap, thought Castle, who stood with arms folded, fingering the brim of his new fedora and watching.

"Mr. Castle? Gene Castle, is it?"

The guy had that dashing, insouciant air that Castle didn't

123

care for at all, probably because he had little of it himself. On this one it wasn't as bad as it might have been because he was short, and didn't know how to dress. Consequently, there was none of the vainglorious about him. He needed a shave and his suit needed a pressing. It was probably a good thing the suit needed a pressing, Castle thought, because it didn't even begin to fit the guy. If it was clean and pressed and didn't fit, he'd look ridiculous. The knot of his tie was down around the third button of his shirt and a grey fedora was pushed back on wavy black hair that the lucky bastard never had to comb. There was a press card stuck in his hatband. Castle recalled seeing him just the other day, looking down at Henry the Hype and taking notes.

"Who wants to know?"

"Joe Frontenac of the *Times*."

"The hard-living, daredevil ace reporter?"

"Yeah, that's me, and I'd like to ask you a few questions."

"Oh, would you now?"

"Yeah, did you and Harry Greene have an argument recently?"

"I knew Harry Green twenty-five years and never had an argument with him."

"What happened that last time you saw Harry Greene?"

"He didn't do a damned thing. Just lay there on the wharf in a pool of blood, a halo of the same red stuff around his head. You get a kick out of asking these questions?"

"It's my job."

"Sure. Why don't you go ask the widow how she feels?"

"I already did, this morning. You had an appointment with him?"

"That's right. He left the message with the switchboard operator. I didn't even get a chance to speak to him on the phone."

"Is it true that you're working for the WUA as a private investigator?"

"What would they need a private investigator sneaking around for? Find out who says nasty things about Lenin outside the office?"

"How'd you get the split lip and the cut head? Cops work you over?"

"No, sir. I fell off the roof of a whorehouse."

"Sure."

Castle shrugged his shoulders.

"It would have been worse but I met something with ears shaped like teardrops on the way down. It broke my fall with its paws. You can quote me on that."

"Thanks. How'd you get along with Alex Tremaine?"

"Only met the fellow once. All we did was exchange hello, how you doing, and if I need a witness to that, there he is over there with a satisfied look on his mug."

His speech finished, Finnegan had left the platform and was passing nearby with his own gaggle of followers.

Frontenac called his name. Finnegan looked but didn't have to be waved over. His expression turned to righteous anger when he spotted Castle.

"Did Castle and Tremaine have an argument?"

"I introduced them at the office. They didn't say much of anything to each other. But..." Finnegan stole a glance at Castle, "I don't know what might have occurred later. If you want to ask him meaningful questions, why don't you start with what he was doing at ten o'clock last night? And why the cops have Alex and not him?"

"The cops already asked me where I was at ten o'clock. The cops must know something you don't know, junior. But since we're all playing detective, why don't you tell me what my motive would be for killing a guy I'd known for twenty-five years without a cross word passing between us? Or any kind of word in four years since that was the last time we saw each when both of us were alive?"

The crowd seemed to be making more noise now.

125

Finnegan chewed his lower lip and looked at the ground. Finally, he glanced at Castle long enough to utter one word, "Guilt."

"Guilt. Pretty lame. About what?"

"For selling out."

"Uh huh. Selling out to whom? Hell, if I had to kill someone because I was feeling guilty about my politics, or lack thereof, I could have killed you."

The union people began to chant, "Free Tremaine!"

Immediately their opponents attempted to shout them down.

"Come to think of it, Finnegan. With Harry dead and Tremaine in the lock-up, you're the big shot at the WUA now. Acting Chairman. Could such a thing have happened under any other circumstance? Got your own little retinue now to give orders to. Maybe one of the frails will fall for your righteous demeanor."

"What exactly are you implying?"

"I just implied it exactly."

"Finnegan?" Frontenac broke in, "is Castle here working for the WUA?"

"I'd hardly call it working."

Dozens of voices roared a single word: "Three!"

With that a group of protesters rushed the City Hall steps. There was a line of cops on the landing at the top of the steps, and every third one broke rank and started down. Cops and protesters met halfway and started to battle. There was more fighting at the bottom of the stairs between union sympathizers and their opponents. A group of thugs took after a man with a picket sign. They cut him out of the group like cattle rustlers. He kept a hold on his sign like it was a holy relic. He ran with it and clasped it to himself even after they'd caught up and knocked him down. Protected it while they kicked him in the ribs and in the head.

From each side of City Hall, the mounted police began

126

moving outwards, as if inscribing a circle on the lawn. As they did so, a phalanx of cops formed and started toward the stairs. To Castle, an observer from beyond the circle of horseman, it seemed like a massive public ballet. Each horseman took hold of his billyclub, each cop on the ground already had his in hand. These latter started up the stairs. Their partners on the landing started down. And in a moment both lines were swinging and their victims were screaming.

"There it is, Finnegan," Castle said. "The test of fire. Look smart now. Your people need you."

Finnegan licked his lips and looked around him. He seemed to sigh before striding, not running, toward the battle. The reporter started after him.

"Hold on Frontenac," Castle called. "I got a question for *you*, When did you hear about them picking up Tremaine?"

"Let's see, a bulletin about the shooting came over the police radio about ten-twenty. I hustled down to the stationhouse right away."

"How long did it take you to get there?"

"Couldn't have taken me more than five minutes. The cub we keep there told me they had a suspect—must have been you. Later I heard there was another guy which would have been Tremaine."

"Uh huh. Let me get this straight. You heard about the shooting over the radio at twenty past ten and by ten twenty-five you were at the stationhouse and had learned there was a suspect in custody. That how it went?"

"Yeah, that's it. Why are you asking me about the exact times? You on to something, Castle?"

Castle didn't answer. He looked over toward city hall. There weren't so many protestors fighting the cops now, most of them were horizontal, sprawled on the steps or on the ground. The horsemen went after anybody not that way, swinging their clubs like scythes. Foot cops prowled among the ones on the ground, if it moved they clubbed or kicked it.

127

"Shame isn't, Frontenac?"

"What's that?"

"Nice new building like that and blood all over the steps. Damn protestors, no more concern for public property than to bleed all over it. You can't wash it away no matter how hard you scrub."

Castle lifted his gaze from the steps.

"What floor is the mayor's office on?"

"Sixth. Why?"

Castle pointed his index finger at City Hall, and counted, moving it upward.

"Seven, eight, nine. Who has offices on the ninth floor?"

"Let's see. Mostly engineering department. Some of the councilmen. What the hell are you looking at?"

"Ninth floor. Direct middle of the tower. Two guys looking out the window. One's in a business suit, the other's..."

"Wait. Yeah, I see them. The other guy's dressed in some sort of uniform."

"Uh huh. That cap, he's wearing, look's like an admiral. You think the other guy could be a councilman? Can you make him out?"

"No, it's too dark, there's a glare."

"Yeah. The other one, in a uniform like that, if he ain't an admiral, and I'm not saying admirals don't hang out at City Hall, but if he ain't, what is he? Dressed like that? If it's not the fire chief, then it might be....who?"

"Wilkins?"

"Yeah, Wilkins, our highly respected Chief of Police. How about that, eh? Frontenac, wait just a second. Where you off to? What's the rush all of a sudden? The head bashing's in the other direction."

"I got a story to write. I mean the Chief of Police at City Hall in a councilman's office, the day of a riot?"

"I don't know, Frontenac."

Castle was looking up there. "That window is real big, and

the two of them don't fill it. I got a feeling there's someone missing from the picture. Maybe this someone's in the background pulling the levers."

"Well, what the hell. I don't know whether I should try to sneak into City Hall, get back to my office and write what I got, or follow you."

"Don't worry, I got an idea we'll meet again."

With that, Castle turned away.

"Where you going?"

"No where you'd be interested in following me. I'm gonna get drunk and then I'm gonna read the encyclopedia."

Chapter Eighteen

Castle stopped the Plymouth outside the green door on Hastings Street beyond which the stairs lead to the Manhattan Club. It was a quarter past three in the afternoon, the rain had stopped and the street was packed. A man held his kid's hand, the boy wearing his baseball cap, and they were making in the direction of Woodward's where Pop was probably going to buy junior a bat with Jimmy Foxx's autograph on it. Castle thought about having a kid and a decent job and working half-days on Saturday and when he came out of the office or the plant, there'd be the little scamp waiting for him, eagerness and hero worship all over his face. They'd go down to the sandlot and he'd hit a few out to the boy. His son. A goofy mutt who wanted to get into the act and who'd retrieve the stray balls, slobbering all over them, was all that was needed to complete the picture. The mutt should have a black circle around its eye, and there should never be rain on Saturday afternoons. Yeah, he thought, I need that drink, bad.

When he came out it was nighttime, it was raining again,

and people moved differently, with a kind of urgency, like there were only a few hours left and they had to fill them with fun, damn it. Of course, he moved differently too, and he wasn't even drunk. He lit his last cigar, opened the door of the Plymouth and sat down heavily on soaked upholstery. It hadn't been raining six hours ago and he had rolled down both windows. Actually, it didn't feel all that bad; invigorating, kind of.

Castle looked in the rear view mirror, first thing, like all good drivers do—he must be feeling the effects of the booze somewhat because he was very much aware of trying to act like good drivers do. He saw a trolley and trucks and cars all framing his face. It was almost like the traffic in the rear view mirror was avoiding his mug, detouring around it, and little could he blame the traffic. Tough and tired was the way he looked; too tired to be tough was the way he felt. He pulled out.

"What the hell," he said out loud. "What the *hell* am I doing driving down the main stem of this sodden honkytonk town with a single sawbuck in my pocket on a woebegone Saturday night when I should be on a yacht in the Mediterranean with Lila Damita watching Lila stretch way up, then bend all the way over, as she hauls on the halyard, and reaches way over there for the button that brings the waiter, Paco from Pamplona—with our liquid refreshment. Ah, the Mediterranean... Trieste, where I'd promise never to be sad... Ravello from the terrace, over biscotti soaked with anisette and a bowl of strong coffee on a sober morning... St. Paul de Vance and Countess what-*was*-her-name?... but most of all I remember the blue waters of Naples and how the sunlight glinted off the white villas there on the hills that day we sailed for Abyssinia the first time. Italy. What *is* it about Italy?"

Though he stopped the car at a traffic light, Castle kept on talking.

"Garmano. Now why is that name familiar? Or, is it fami-

131

iliar? I don't know what I know anymore. Hell, I ought to quit this kind of thing, go into partnership with Charlie-boy. Be respectable-like, get into that export business, exporting the scared, the frightened and the doomed back to Uncle Adolf... Garmano..."

"Hey!"

Castle nearly hit his head on the roof. The voice belonged to the woman who was leaning into the opened passenger-side window. She had on too much makeup but she was decidedly not unattractive, expecially with her little breasts almost completely revealed by the low cut blouse. They swayed—her little breasts—gently to the rhythm of the motor, only the nipples hiding from sight.

"Wake up, big boy. It's against the law to drive while you're talking in your sleep. What d'you say we go to a party, eh? There'll be lots of booze and hot music and plenty of messing around."

"Oh, yeah? And who'll be there, luscious?"

"Why just you and me, and I'm a pushover."

"Sounds smashing but, alas, I got something on for tonight."

"Yeah, what?"

"I'm going back to my office, sit at my desk and read the encyclopedia. Going to read about Italy."

The light changed and a car behind honked impatiently.

"Jeez, a weirdo," the woman said, backing away from the Plymouth. "You been smoking those muggles, mister?"

"See you, doll," Castle said letting the clutch out.

"Yeah," she called after him. "Try to keep your hands on top of the desk, eh?"

132

Castle pulled off the main stem and the faded tawdriness of midnight, onto the limbo of Columbia Street, and into the dark lane of forlorn delivery trucks, overflowing trash cans, crouching cats and smooching Indians. Beyond the loading ramps, he turned into the garage and crept past the shapes of angle parked cars to his personal spot at the back. He got out and slammed shut the door. He thought his footsteps sounded loud. There was no other sound.

Castle turned out of the garage and there was no cat or rat scratching through garbage; he could hear no panting nor snap of brassiere in the night but he listened out of habit. There was nothing save for the vague hum of traffic a couple of blocks away.

Nothing until he heard that particular noise that is only made when tires roll slowly, crunching gravel.

Castle dove behind the trash cans and machine gun fire shattered the stillness, potting the bricks of the garage wall. The three metal cans hid him, curled up like a baby and saying novenas. Looking between the cans, he saw his brand new fedora in the middle of the alley and as well he saw the barrel of the gun that was pointing out of the back window of a sedan inching along. He reached back for the revolver in the waist band of his pants, there at the small of his back, raised it above the tops of the cans and let off three shots. The answering fire made the gravel dance and beat a tattoo across the cans, stunning his eardrums. He pushed the revolver away from him, after promising to say the novenas for all nine days if things went his way, and stretched out with his feet exposed. Castle lay still.

There was more crunching of gravel and after a long moment, he heard it ping against the undercarriage of the sedan as the driver accelerated. The automobile moved away and the motor strained in first gear. He heard the shift into second and soon the sound of the automobile was gone. Still he waited. He lay there for another minute before standing up, retrieving his gun and his hat. He walked away, brushing off his clothes. There was a bullet hole in his new hat but, Castle told himself, he'd be damned if he'd buy another one.

Chapter Nineteen

Castle was asleep, the covers pulled up over his head like he was hiding, his arms had the pillow in a bear hug. But it was not the sleep of the dead or the innocent because the sound of the door knob being worked from the outside woke him. He was aware of pale morning sunlight coming in through the window and of the fact that his right hand, which was underneath the pillow and on top of the revolver, was numb.

There was a rattling in the lock. The knob turned and the door began to open while Castle was slowly switching hands. He got the gun into his left and pointed it at the doorway.

Louise Jones stood there holding her suitcase.

"Now that's the kind of greeting I like. A man with his pistol ready."

Castle sank back onto the mattress and felt the tension drain from his body.

"How you doing, Louise?"

"Just hunky-dory," she said, putting down the suitcase. "Mandrake the Magician and his sidekick, the lovely Louise Latour, wowed them at the Palace and the Hi Hat Club. But what the hell happened to you, you look awful. Been sparring with the Brown Bomber?"

"No, I fell off a roof."

"Oh."

"Finally, someone who believes me."

"Whose roof was it?" Louise asked, getting out of her coat.

"Roof of a whorehouse"

"Oh, yeah? What were you doing there?"

"Getting beat up by three goons."

Louise shook her head.

"I go away for a few days and your tastes change completely."

"They beat me up and *then* they threw me off the roof."

"Makes it spicier that way. That all that happened?"

"Let's see. There was a pete job. I met Jesus's cousin, two hookers were abducted, somebody murdered Harry Greene, I dodged forty-five or fifty machine gun bullets last night, and I've been walking around in a funhouse maze trying to figure out who did what and what it means."

"You should be glad I'm back, add some excitement to your humdrum existence."

"I am glad you're back. Why don't you come over here and let me show you."

"Sure, kid, but you got to get rid of one of those things that's pointing at me."

Castle dropped the revolver to the floral patterned carpet, and Louise came toward him rolling her hips, and got into bed with all her clothes on.

They were still in bed an hour later and Louise still had her skirt on. Her undergarments, however, were hanging on a bed-post. There was a pillow between her back and the headboard and she was smoking a cigarette. Castle lay next to her with the sheet pulled up to his waist.

"So you think all these events are connected?"

"Uh huh. But who, or what, is connecting them, I don't know. If the bulls brought me in when they already had Tremaine—which they did—it means they were trying to make a show. But for who and why? And this Tremaine? Have I seen him before? And Garmano, who the hell is he? How come him and his boys were waiting for me when I got to the room with the girl? And I can't get over the picture I have in my mind of the police chief and some other guy in the city hall window."

"I got a feeling you got a feeling what's behind it all after all."

"I got a feeling you're right."

"But, if I know you, you're not going to tell me because you're superstitious."

"Yeah, you know me."

"Okay, so just tell me one little thing. As far as you knew, it was just going to be you and the beautiful English girl in that room. After you got the information you wanted were you going to..."

There was a knock on the door and Castle reached across Louise and got the gun from the floor. He gestured to her and she called out, "Who is it?"

A Chinese voice answered, "Have message for Mr. Castle. Urgent."

Louise swung her legs off the bed. "Who's it from?"

"From Mister Johnny, old man."

Castle motioned with the gun and Louise stepped to the side of the door and opened it. The guy who came into the room was wearing slippers, a silk pyjama suit and a coolie hat. He bowed first to Louise and then to Castle. He straightened up and removed his hat. His hair was plastered down and parted in the middle.

"Morning, Louise. You can hide the heater, Gene. It's me, Sammy Ah."

"You had me there, Sammy. You look real quaint. Got your rickshaw with you?"

"You know me, Gene," Sammy smiled. "Dealing from the bottom or a little Pai Gow in the Wah On Rooms on Saturday night is the most work I ever do."

Sammy's expression turned serious.

"Johnny needs to talk to you, Gene. He sent for me because he says you got to get in without Garmano's goons seeing you. He says it's real important. I'll leave now. You hurry and get dressed and then go into Fong's laundry. The guy there'll show you to the back. Oh, yeah, you got a dirty shirt?"

"Plenty of them over there in the closest. Take one, you need it."

"Always the joker. Bring one with you, make it look right. You ever been underneath Shanghai Alley?"

"Kick the gong around when I was a kid."

"You ain't seen nothin yet. I'll go now."

Sammy put on his coolie hat, bowed, winked and departed.

It was only few blocks away but a long walk when someone needed you. A long walk to drop off a dirty shirt. Couple of minutes and he was turning south onto Main Street. Up ahead at the intersection was Irish Tony Doyle, carrying his little cloth bag, just come from the newly opened Eastern Sports Centre, a block away.

"Hiya, Castle. How ya doin, huh?"

"Irish. You in training again?"

"Best shape of my life," Irish Tony snuffled. "Making a comeback, fighting some Eyetalian at the Grandview Arena next week. Be there, bud."

138

"Sure thing."

The guy's nose had been broken so many times, his breath had to follow a route with as many curves as a logging road through the Coast Mountains, and he wheezed and gasped like an old truck at every switchback.

"I win, McLarnin says he'll get me onna undercard with him at the Garden in New York."

"Way to go. Sounds like that could be the big break."

Thirty-seven years old, he'd already had two hundred fights, officially; and won a few more than half of them. Sure he was dreaming but what else was there? Wait tables? He couldn't breathe well enough to stay on his feet for more than three minutes at a time. Had to knock the other guy out before the fifth or it was all over.

"Just a couple of days til the big fight. Eh, Gene?"

"Yeah, the Kraut's just a stepping stone for Louis."

"Yeah. See you around."

Castle continued along Main Street. Couple of blocks too many. He should change hotels. There was the Brazil over there, and the Arco. But he liked keeping some distance between himself and the office. A flat or apartment, forget it. You stayed in Vancouver, unless you had family and a regular job, most times you lived in a hotel. It was a tradition and it made sense. It was a transient, seasonal town; people went away and did a job of work; or they did a job of work and went away. In between times, they had these places that catered to you. Most of them were clean and the management knew you. It wasn't like that in other cities. More like a big family, is what Castle told himself. But, as is usually the case, the family members some times didn't treat each other right.

He turned west on Pender Street and now everything was Chinese. There was Tommy's brother's hotel, the Ah Chew. Once he tried to explain to Tommy why he found the name funny but Tommy didn't understand, or he understood but didn't see the humour. Tommy said his people made a different sound. They went, "FFrruuffh!" Call it the FFrruuffh! Hotel, that would be funny. Different customs, Tommy said; we're all living here mixed up together and ain't it nice?

Maybe he should get a new office instead of new living quarters. But, he couldn't do that. He'd miss Laura and working next to Beanie Brown; but most of all, he liked being across from the Alley, the first place in the country, the Chinese people had settled. And he liked looking down there to the end of the Alley and seeing the big ships. There was usually one there and you could think of how things might be in some other place. Sure, there was always the individual who would inform you it was the same wherever you went. The things that mattered were always the same, is what they said. They were probably right, too. But so what?

"Riot at City Hall!"

You could hear the little man with the big voice from half a block away, from the Chinese Daily News building, at least. When Castle had closed that half-a-block, Woody said, "Here's your paper, Gene. What's that? You find a shirt on the street?"

"Uh huh. Real fashionable one it is. Has its own collar. Take it over to Fong's, get the tread marks cleaned out of it, I'll be ready to do the town. You want, I'll look around for one for you."

"Yeah, look for one with some extra room in the back for my hump. Say, that Frontenac done another of his I-Was-Theres."

Woody took the money and gave Castle his paper, saying, "You see the way he starts off his story, 'Blood on the steps of city hall. Blood that won't wash away.'Kinda dramatic, ain't it?"

"Yeah. Real original too. Frontenac reminds me of Richard Harding Davis."

"Who's that?"

"Some bum I met in Nicaragua. Speaking of bums, that guy

across the street. How long's he been planted there?"

"I come to the corner six o'clock, he's here. There's another guy halfway down the Alley. Coupla times a day, they get replaced by other guys. They buy their papers from me. Don't say nuthin, not even a 'top of the morning, guvnor,' nuthin like that. They just grunt. Think guys like that can even read?"

"Not the big one over there. He just buys it so he can have something to look over the top of."

"Jesuits taught me to read up near Williams Lake. My mother tried to do right by me, sending me to school and all. Most of the other kids were out in the bush with their old man learning to hunt and fish and trap. I never learned none of that but I learned to read. I think they got the best of the deal."

"Guess it depends."

"Yeah. Be seein you, Gene...Riot At City Hall...Blood On the Steps...Streetfight in Barcelona!"

Castle crossed the street, paper in hand, dirty shirt over his arm, and went into Fong's Laundry.

Tiny bells tinkled as he opened and closed the door. A Chinese man and a white lady were discussing the pile of laundry on the counter between them. The man glanced at Castle before making a final count of the articles of clothing.

Behind the man, to either side of a door in the wall, were shelves with laundry wrapped in neat brown paper packages. The smell of starch and soap, the sound of washing machines and pressing machines, filled the air.

The woman took her laundry ticket and left the store. When the door had closed, the man pointed to the door in the wall. Castle went behind the counter and the man stepped toward him, smiled and took his shirt.

Sammy Ah was waiting on the other side of the door in the large work room. Sammy Ah in his usual garb, suit and tie-stick, pin under the knot, lifting it up.

Men and women were at machines. There were stainless

141

steel sinks larger than any he had ever seen. The two halves of the pressing machines reminded him of French rolls; when the operator pulled a lever, the top and the bottom closed together like they were making a sandwich of a pair of pants.

Nobody appeared to pay any attention to the white man in their midst nor did they look up when Sammy pushed aside one of the laundry hampers, a big basket on a wheeled trolley, and peeled back a rubber mat, exposing a door in the wooden floor. Sammy lifted the door and stepped down onto a ladder, bidding Castle to follow.

Fourteen steps and Sammy Ah was waiting for him in what was probably a storage room but it was too dark for Castle to make anything out except for shelving and cabinets. Sammy felt around on the wall next to a cabinet.

"Here it is," he said, and the row of shelves slid away.

They stepped into a dark narrow hallway, the only light from a dim bulb on a cross beam that Castle had to duck under. After ten or so yards, the passage opened onto a room where Chinese men sat at a table playing cards. The men didn't look up as they went around them and found another door that lead to another dark hallway.

"So you've never seen this, eh?"

"No. Is Shanghai Pete's around here?"

Sammy Ah laughed.

"That's for suckers. Pete peddles the mystery of the orient jazz to the round eyes, nickel a point. You got a guy sells insurance all week, he wants to get away from the missus of a Saturday night, and he's heard about Pete's, right? So Pete brings him under the alley, the sucker takes a gander, wonders if he's gotten in over his head. Which he has, in more ways than one. Soon's he's worrying all these inscrutable yellow fellows are going to blow opium in his face and he'll wake up wrapped in rope in the hold of a junk on the South China Sea. Can't play good cards in that frame of mind which is precisely the point."

"Just a high class gaff-joint."

"A high class skibo gaff joint. Now look in here."

Sammy made a part in a beaded curtain that reminded Castle of the one in his office but there were never any slinky dolls in evening gowns serving drinks in his office.

"This is where we take the tripod off," Sammy declared, in a whisper.

Four men were seated at a lacquered table staring at little enamel blocks, the size of match boxes, that each had in front of him. A young Chinese man stood against a wall behind the gamblers, arms folded over his dinner jacket. He looked like he knew a hundred esoteric ways to bend and twist your body so it would hurt real bad.

"You got to show a thousand clams to sit down in there," Sammy whispered. "And the *heavy* action is in some of the other rooms. But let's not tary."

Halfway along another hall, a boy emerged from a room holding a tray. Through a crack in the doorway, Castle got a glimpse of Chinese men lying on their hips in bunks, sucking at the mouthpieces of water pipes. There was another boy in there tending to the pipes, preparing the balls of opium. Some of the men looked dead.

"Brings back old memories of being on the hip," Castle said.

"Some of them are so hip they're gone."

They came to another open area but this one was nearly the size of a city block, and dirt—thick black soil—covered the ground. Through the middle of the big space was a raised walkway of wooden planks. On one side of the walk, young plants were visible, green shoots sticking out of the soil. On the other side were mounds of earth and peat.

"What's the hell's going on here?" Castle asked, following Sammy on the walkway.

Sammy pointed left, pointed right. "Bean sprouts, mushrooms."

When they had crossed the open area, Sammy stopped, reached toward the ceiling and pulled down a ladder.

Johnny stood in the doorway of his room and watched the little door under the stairs open and a hand reach out and push at May's wagon. Limping across the hall, he moved the wagon and held the door for Sammy Ah. Gene Castle came out behind him.

"Well I'll be damned."

He saw that Johnny's eyes were red, and looked over his shoulder to where the old lady lay motionless on the bed.

"What's the matter with May?"

"Nothin now, lad. She's dead."

"Oh, no, Johnny."

"Yeah."

"What happened?"

"Let's go in the room."

"I'll leave now," said Sammy Ah. "Call me if you need me."

"Okay," said Johnny, his voice a rough murmur. "I appreciate it, Sammy."

The man nodded and disappeared into the opening under the staircase.

They went into the room.

"Sit down, Gene. Wherever you can make room."

Johnny lowered himself onto the stool near his banjo and Castle went around to the other side of the bed. He took some old magazines off a kitchen chair and straddled it so his chest was resting against the back support. They faced each other across May's body, Johnny holding one of her hands in both of his.

"I saw in the paper where they picked you up for Harry's murder and let you go. Saw that they nabbed this other fellow. Well he didn't do it."

"Tremaine? How do you know that?"

"Because I was there."

"You were *there*?" Castle felt peculiar, talking with May like that between them. "What do you mean you were there?"

"I was there, is what I mean. Me and May."

He patted the lifeless hand in his hands.

"We saw the whole thing. Listen, you remember a guy—this is going back before your time but you might of heard of him —guy named Scarbani? Pushy they called him."

"Scarbani. Pushy Scarbani. I don't know, the nickname makes it familiar somehow."

"Used to work for the bosses. A contract thug on loan out of Denver."

Johnny's voice came on like a lonesome train.

"You might connect his name to the Winnipeg General Strike back in '19. He came up and helped put that down, working for Lyle, you know, the bastard that later shot himself and his wife. He used to like, this Scarbani did, to push guys off the top of buildings or cliffs, bridges, like that. Got a big thrill out of doing that. How he got his nickname."

"You knew the guy?"

"Yeah, I knew him. He'd get into these groups and sometimes take out the leaders. Kill them if he had to but more often he just hurt them, sometimes forever. Give you an example. There was this one fellow. Scarbani and a couple of his buddies tied this fellow up, took him up on a railway bridge in Washington State and then they pushed him off. Guy fell about seventy-five feet. Landed on a gravel bar. Kind of thing he used to like to do."

Castle looked into the old man's red rimmed eyes. "That fellow was you. Wasn't it?"

"Yeah, that was me. And Scarbani, him and his buddies, they took bets before they pushed me."

"Bets? What d'you mean, they took bets?"

"Took bets on whether I'd live or not."

145

Castle looked glumly at his hands that hung down over the back of the chair; looked at May, the sheet and tattered blanket tucked around her mummy form.

"What about Harry Greene?" he finally said.

"Hold on a minute. I got to tell you more about this Scarbani. One guy he did kill was the Vice-President of Keystone Iron and Steel. But he did it by mistake. He was supposed to knockoff the Doc, Rose's old pal; your buddy. They sent him to the plant in Wheeling where the Doc had gone over some lock-out business. The Doc met with Franck, the Vice-President, as part of a grievance committee and Scarbani had gotten in there. He pulled his gun calmly as you please and fired. But who he plugged was Franck. The Doc looked so respectable that Scarbani must of figured, that guy can't be no radical."

"So you might say this Pushy, he made an *honest* mistake."

"Yeah, it was a favour he done the radical movement. Anyway, Pushy had to get out of the country. He went back to Italy and palled out Mussolini around the time Mussolini had just finished leading the march on Rome. Anyway when Mussolini got in the government, he made a big show of going up against what they call the Mafia. One of his men says to him, 'Who're you going to use to fight these men; they're bad men.' Mussolini says, 'I'm going to use worse men.'

"So what Mussolini done, he got people from Calabria —from the old time crime people because these others are from Sicily, and they hate each other.

"Time goes by, Pushy he gets in trouble with Mussolini, running his own games. When he skipped out of the country he had a half a million dollars on him, money he managed to score of when Il Duce drained the marshes around Rome."

"The Pontine marshes. One of those mass fascist work projects. Done with slave labour practically."

"Yeah, that's the name. So Pushy disappears and shows up in Africa. He went there to break some guys out of jail.

146

Two, maybe more guys. It's school time, Gene. What country in Africa?"

"I got a feeling it's one I've been to lately."

"Uh huh, and these guys caught a ship. You know the name of the Calabrian crime fraternity, then you know where the guys got off the ship."

Castle looked blankly at Johnny for a moment before astonishment started playing around with his features as he puzzled the thing out. He looked at Johnny whose grin was macabre, maniacal, his broken teeth and almost yellow gums.

"You just remembered what they're called."

"Uh huh."

"So they landed, poor immigrants fleeing the bogeyman over there. So you know who it was had Harry Greene shot."

Castle nodded, "And you saw the whole thing."

"I saw it. We saw it, May and I. But him and his boys saw us. We tried to get away but it was no use."

Johnny looked at May's lifeless hand, all bones and hard blue veins, and he stroked it tenderly.

"He knocked my girl down, broke her arm. She was all busted up inside from the fall. I asked him to kill us but he said he wouldn't 'for old times sake.' Yeah, for a little torture like in the good old days. You know I never ratted out anybody, no matter what. It's a habit. Back when I was with the Wobblies, you think we ever went to the bulls? We always figured there was some way we could even things up with whatever bastards it was that done us. It might take a week or a year but we usually got our own back. But this Pushy, he hurt her just for the hell of it. He's had these guys watching the place ever since. With May dead, I got nothing to live for. I'm going to sing about the whole thing. It's the only way I got of getting back at him. In case something happens to me, I wanted one person I could trust to know what's going on. Maybe you can help me state my case."

"Hold on, Johnny. Think on this for a while. Why did he

break May's arm? He wanted a hold on you. Why are the boys watching? He's waiting to see you out on the street a few times without May. If he knows she's dead, his goons are going to follow their guns in here and blast you far away."

"Hell I care about that?"

"You got to be alive to tell your story, and they got to think May's alive, to keep you that way."

"I must be a step or two behind you."

"Look, this guy's smart. He's inside your head. He knows what you're thinking whatever the situation. He thinks, if May's dead, you're going to sing because nothing else matters. He knows there's no way you'd sing otherwise."

"Okay, I see it now."

"You don't like the bulls, eh Johnny?"

"Come on, Gene. What the hell."

"Yeah. Well it's nice you can't sing to them anyway."

"You lost me again."

"They're in this. At the very top. The way it looks, the bad guys and the good guys, they've gotten together and their plan is to bust the unions. They do that and there's no more Commie menace to spook the big money. There won't any malcontents screaming for relief. All that stuff. Hell, if the fat cats think it can be done in British Columbia, where there is always what the papers call labour strife and unrest, then they'll try it in the other provinces and the people down south will get the same idea. But, most of all, back east they'll start thinking for once that they can invest a little out here and get a whole lot back without worrying that the poor slobs are going to start sticking up for what they insist are their rights. Then we'll see this land grow and prosper. Business, bub. Yessiree, it's business that makes this country great."

"Yeah, sure."

"I can see the wondrous future. Glory be."

"Yeah, Gene. Look, I got another question for you. You know who the guy was that Pushy, or Augie, as he calls him self now, the guy he brought to Canada with him was?"

"Yeah," Castle nodded. "I've known for about two minutes. Same guy that stole the twenty thousand from the WUA."

"It's his half-brother."

Johnny placed May's hand at her side.

"There's just one thing but it's the big thing. How we going to make them think May's still alive?"

"I think I got that figured out."

Chapter Twenty

Sammy Ah took one of Johnny's arms and Gene Castle, the other, as they helped him up through the little door under the staircase and into the hall of the roominghouse. Frank Evans came out last. He had been behind Johnny on the ladder to catch him if he lost his grip. There was also a young Chinese boy with them, a nephew of Sammy's, twelve or thirteen years old.

"Wait...give me a second," Johnny groaned, taking deep breaths. There were tears in his eyes. "Sammy? Sammy, you sure? You sure she's going to be all right down there?"

"Johnny, our most venerated ancestors are down there. My mother is buried there."

"Are you ready now, Johnny?" Castle spoke. "I got to remind you what I said before: this is going to be tough on you. It's going to be a shock."

"I know that. I got to do it. Got to face it."

"Now?"

"Yeah, take me in."

It looked as if the body was in the same position. One arm at the side, the other in the splint folded across the chest, scraggly wisps of hair on the pillow, lips drawn back in the hideous grin of death.

They stared at her.

Johnny groaned and took hold of Castle's arm.

The body rose to a sitting position and the eyes opened.

"Jesus, God!"

The old man turned away.

"I'm sorry, Johnny," said the woman, getting up from the bed.

"It's all right. It's all right, Louise."

"We have to get going now," Castle said. "Let's gather up the gear."

"I'll put the stuff in the basket," said Frank.

Louise went out into the hallway, a bent, withered old woman now. There was a gilt-frame mirror on the wall at the foot of the stairs. She looked, felt her face, ran a finger over the rough places where she had shaved her eyebrows, and spoke to her image:

> Where, where pray tell me, is my forehead smooth
> My golden hair, my well-arched eyebrows, too
> And the broad space between my sparkling eyes?
> Where is that look, a torch to man's desire,
> That made the wisest sage become a fool?
> Where is my fine, straight nose, each tiny ear,
> My dimpled chin, those features clear and fine,
> And, to tempt all, those beautiful red lips?

Louise turned away from the mirror and stared at a spot on the wallpaper at the far end of the hall.

> Those sweet, slim shoulders, I remember them well,
> Those long, soft arms, those slender hands,

151

Those tender, little breasts and hips so firm,
So high and lovely and enticing, they
So excellent for love, his tourneys dear,
Where in its place that lovely jewel lay
Resting enshrined in its fair setting there
Upon those thighs so generous and lithe.

A door opened across the hallway from Johnny's room, and a young Chinese girl looked out at the hideous old woman talking to herself. Louise turned and faced her, spoke to her:

Now look at me, wrinkled my forehead lies,
Once golden hair (what's left of it) is grey,
Eyebrows are gone and eyes are blear and dull:
Those eyes which once could wound so grievously;
Nose hooked and ugly, shrunken ears hang down,
My mask-like face is lifeless, waxen, dead,
All furrowed my once smooth and rounded chin,
And coarse have once enticing lips become.
And so must end all happiness,
Plump arms are shrivelled, hands withered too,
Bent are my shoulders, and those dainty breasts
All shrunken lie, as do my hips, alas!
As for that jewel fair, oh fie, oh fie!
And now those once fair thighs forlorn do stand,
But thighs no more, just wrinkled flesh and bone,
Withered and thin, speckled like sausage.

Louise knew that the rest of them were in the hall watching her. That the boy had come out first, looked at her and at the girl.

So do we soon regret brief days of joy
And grieve full long, we poor and aged fools,
Grieve as we crouch upon our haunches here

152

Over our little fire of hempen stalks,
So soon alight, so soon a fire no more!

Louise turned her head from the wallpaper, where she had been staring, and glanced at Johnny, at Frank and at her man, fixing her gaze on the young boy for a moment, before looking at the young girl, and nodding.

We that were once so eagerly desired,
So happens it, alack, to one and all.

The girl held the look for a moment. Then she hurriedly went into the room and closed the door.

"Villon," Louise said to the others.

"All right," Castle said. "Let's snap out of it and move. Frank, you grab the basket and help Louise down the steps. Sammy, give Johnny your arm. Don't forget to talk loud enough so the goons can hear you. Okay, Frank?"

"Sure, Gene."

"And, William? You took care of their car?"

"I sneaked under the car while the ugly driver was asleep."

The kid reached into his shopping bag and pulled out a distributor cap with spark plug wires dangling from it.

"Good. That's a trick they'll understand."

"Let's get it over with,"said Johnny.

Castle opened the front door for them and stepped aside. "I can't let them see me so I'll stay here."

He turned to Louise, "Break a leg, kid."

"Thanks. Just what I need."

They left the rooming house; Frank helping Louise; followed by Johnny, Sammy Ah and William. Stepping between a push cart and a truck with Chinese characters on the side, they crossed the street to Sammy Ah's roadster parked outside the Gee Yim barbershop.

When he saw the guy grab the old lady's elbow and help

her into the back seat of the car, Garmano's gorilla figured something was going on that he ought to observe closely

"Give me your hand, dearie," he heard Frank say. He was the kind of jerk you saw sitting in the door of a boxcar going to pick peaches.

"Here you are, then. You'll like it on the farm."

And the old lady, she says, "I don't like farms. I grew up on a ranch."

Big deal, Marco told himself; instead of horse crap you got to step in goat crap.

"It's a nice farm, May," said Johnny. This guy, Marco thought, the one the boss talked to the other night, he is old enough to have had gnocchi with Garibaldi. The old lady's carping about having to go to the farm, and he's saying, "Fresh air. Your arm'll heal up in no time." Like he's trying to talk her into please going. In the old country, Pop told Mama to get in the car—what am I saying? Marco asked himself; I mean the, what do you call it in English? The wagon the donkey pulls? —the carretto asino, and in she went, no lip. You even looked at Pop the wrong way, he belted you.

"So long's I don't have to milk no cows."

Don't worry, old lady, Marco told her in his head. The cow's, they're gonna run away and jump the goddamned fences, they see you coming.

The old man was in the back seat with the old lady now, and he put his arm around her. Maybe he was gonna kiss her; Mary and Joseph, what a sight that would be. Then the hobo got in the car and the Chink got behind the wheel. The little Chink kid, wiping the car off with a rag. They let a Chink drive a nice car like that.

"In a week you'll be good as new and we'll come back to town."

I bet new wasn't so hot.

The Chink asked them if they wanted him to put the top up.

"Hell, no," said the old lady. "I want to feel the wind in

154

my hair."

And just as Marco was thinking—What hair?; the old broad said, "What's left of it."

The roadster pulled away from the curb and all the Chinese moved out of the way, the way those people move, like crabs. They know what's going on but they don't ever let on. Marco walked out into the middle of the street and watched after the car. He decided he better go back and tell Vince what happened.

Vince was asleep.

"Huh?" he growled, as Marco shook him. "What?"

Marco pointed down Shanghai Alley.

"Hell you pointing at?"

"They got in a car. The old man and the old lady and a guy and a Chink and they drove away. You think we ought to follow them?"

"Yeah. I guess we gotta. Get in."

Marco went around to the passenger's side and Vince pressed the starter button. Nothing happened. He pressed again.

"*Pastari*! Look under the hood."

Marco got out, lifted one side of the winged hood and stared at the engine compartment.

"Yeah?"

Marco shrugged.

"Look on the other side."

Marco went around and the raised the other wing.

"Well?" called Vince impatiently. The guy stood there like he was in Firenze staring at paintings.

"Uh," Marco began, "I don't know much about cars."

"*Festucci!*"

Vince got out, slammed the car door, had a look and said the word again, "*Festucci.*"

Marco was on the other side of the car. "There's usually a lot more wires, aren't there?"

155

"Yeah, there're usually a lot more wires," Vince mimicked him. "But they ain't there no more."

Marco leaned over the engine, as if trying to find where the wires were hiding.

"*Pastari!*" Vince spit and slammed down his side of the hood.

"*Pastari!*" he cursed again, slamming down the other wing.

"Ahhh!" Marco shrieked, as the wing closed on his fingers. "Ahhh! *Pazzo!*"

Vince returned the insult. Marco cursed Vince, and kicked the car to emphasize his point. They cast aspersions on each other's village back in Calabria, hollered general imprecations and waved their hands while fifty Chinese people went around them without looking at them.

Chapter Twenty-One

The man could afford to live just about anywhere in town that he wished. He could have one of those huge imitaton-Tudor mansions in Shaughnessy with a genuine British butler and an authentic Japanese gardener, or in a modern joint with lots of glass on the water at Point Grey, keep his yacht tied up outside the door. But that would be dumb, living like that, suspicious, and Councilman Miller was not dumb. That was why he lived in the perfectly respectable and perfectly dull area called Marpole with street after street of neat little homes and closely cropped lawns, which you better keep closely cropped or you'd have the Neighborhood Betterment Committee to deal with. Viewed from the sky, from an aeroplane rented with pilot by the half-hour at the flying field just two miles away on the other side of the Fraser River—maybe you've taken your girl up there, quicken her pulse—what Marpole looks like is the faces of a huge waffle iron.

Councilman Miller had organized that Committee that kept the lawns cropped, the houses painted and the East sawmill workers away. In Marpole, the head of the house worked, for goodness sake. There were plenty of jobs out there, whatever they said about a Depression, if a fellow had the grit and determination to get off his duff and find them. Standing behind the man with the job was the homemaker. You saw her, usually in the kitchen with the crisp apron on, her hair up in a bun, cooking a wholesome dinner that the breadwinner deserved after a hard day at the office or the plant. The homemaker, when she had to go into town, didn't loiter on the pavements or linger at Woodward's counter smoking cigarettes and gossiping with the types of women around there. She couldn't do that, not with a hubby, two kids who'd be getting back from school any minute, and a house-hold to manage. That was for another kind of woman; Councilman Miller smirked, thinking of that other kind.

Ralph honked the taxi's horn at seven-thirty, as he did every weekday morning, and Councilman Miller left his neat little house. He was the breadwinner but Gladys never got up in the mornings to make his breakfast. Who'd want to see her anyway, that time of day, hair in curlers, cream all over her face, cigarette breath? She sat there on the edge of the bed with her legs crossed and the cotton between her fat toes, keeping them apart, as she painted the nails red. The hell with her, he thought, who needs her.

Ralph's obsequious way of saying good morning, reminded Councilman Miller that he was a big shot once he closed the front door. He relaxed in the backseat of the cab, looking out the window at the lawns and the houses. Yeah, he could live anywhere he wished and he lived here. They were sure "nice" houses, people said. Which is why, Miller told himself, I own so many of them.

He took some papers from his briefcase and the cab turned north on Cambie Street. The seven year old Plymouth behind it also turned north.

The taxi dropped the councilman off at the White Spot,

half a block from City Hall. Castle waited a couple of minutes before going in. Miller was at the farthest table from the front window with his back to the room. Castle sat at the horseshoe counter which was sectioned off from the table area by a muralled panel. There was the Fraser River with a log boom and several busy boats; along the shore, a steam-chugging locomotive hauled a long line of boxcars and gondolas; an airplane with the Royal Mail circled in the atypical blue sky; over in a corner at the bottom of the painting was the skyline of the bustling city. Castle looked closely but saw no breadlines, no hobos on the boxcars, no jungles in the river weeds.

Looking around the edge of the panel, he could see most of the Councilman. Miller had gotten his breakfast by the time Castle sat down. He must come in every morning. Castle wondered why he didn't eat at home, save him the annoyance of citizens approaching with complaints about the sewers or how they needed a stop sign at their corner, and the neighbors dog peed on their azalea bushes morning and night. That sweet-looking little old lady there was really bending his ear, about how the woman next door—she thinks she's Barbara Stanwyck, that one—is always looking at her through the window. Castle could read her lips. Miller didn't get breakfast at home, maybe he didn't get anything at home which is how come he went to Garmano's establishment. Or maybe there was some other reason.

Twenty minutes later, Miller got up from his table and Castle put the Times in front of his face.

He stared at Jean Hersholt and wondered how they'd cram all The Sins of Man into one movie. The headliner at the Beacon Theatre was Sandy, "The Dog With a Human Mind." Poor doggie, thought Castle, finally getting up from his stool. And I'm the human with a blood hound mind.

Outside, he watched Miller cross Twelfth Avenue, trudge up the front steps and into City Hall.

Castle got his car out of the White Spot lot, drove through

the intersection and parked on Cambie Street. There was a tall laurel hedge running along the edge of the property, on the other side of which was a taxi turnaround and slots for official cars. Castle reasoned that Miller's next appearance would be from this side of the building. The only way he'd come out the front was for another meal at the White Spot. Guys like Miller did business at lunch and they didn't do it in places like that.

Castle read the papers and, every now and again, looked through the bushes. He was afraid he'd see something going on in there and the people involved would see him and think he'd been hoping to see something going on.

He poured coffee from a thermos and studied the "Report from the Training Camps of Both Fighters." He learned that Louis was sure he was going to win and Schmeling was sure he was going to win. The sports reporter ended by wishing good luck to the combatants and expressing his hope that the best man would win.

Done with the *Times*, he read the competition which, on its editorial page, found something good to say about the generals and the priests in Spain who had designs on their democratically elected government. He finished the coffee and turned to the dependable old encylopedia. Still volume seven, *Libido to Mary, Duchess of Burgundy*. It should have been the other way around, the way he figured it. What's the sense of passing the Libido stage long before you got to Mary? He was in the middle of Machiavelli, a misunderstood guy, when Councilman Miller came out and got into a cab that turned down the Cambie Street hill toward the centre of town.

Castle followed, across the bridge and left onto Georgia, west to Burrard and north to Pender where the cab made another left and pulled up in front of the Vancouver Club. Miller got out and went inside. Castle found a parking spot and resigned himself to another wait. He couldn't go in there and sit at the counter, have a coffee and sinker, leave a nickel

160

tip that the waitress would be glad to have. No, the gentlemen in there were the ones who owned all that stuff in the mural at the White Spot. Theirs were the railroads and the land through which the railroads passed, as were the boats on the river, and the logs in the log boom; and the goddamned fish in the river had better jump and spawn when they said jump and spawn. They even claimed the forests and the very mountains, those fellows did; and it was guys like Miller who helped them get a lot of all that. Hey, you want to put a sawmill on the bank right there off Anacis Island but you say you've been told you can't because some old lady with title to all twenty acres won't sell at any price? Don't worry about it, bub. I know this guy at city hall. Of course, it'll take a little grease but, what the hell?

Two hours Miller was in there, and Castle tried to picture him at a table overlooking the inlet, his bland face mounted atop the expensive, conservatively tailored suit, making deals with men who made deals all day, every day, and when they made them they farmed out the details, the work got done and they took their piece without ever actually doing anything except eating and drinking, convincing, cajoling, threatening if need be, and lying through their teeth.

Around two o'clock they began to drift out. Several of the men resembled their caricatures in the old *Wobbly News* or the *New Masses*, and every other left-wing periodical since the beginning of the Industrial Revolution. Looked like butterball turkeys in brown, blue or grey three-piece suits, jackets open, watch chains over bulging bellies. If they spent some time in the steam room, threw the Indian clubs around and shed the pounds, they could cause a crisis among cartoonists of the radical opposition. But, then, there were other ones who looked like they did just that plus play a good deal of tennis. These were the ones that Finnegan and the boys really had to worry about; their money had been lying around multiplying for centuries. Their ancestors had started the prestidigitating

161

in Glaswegian factories way back in the earlies; it was only two generations ago that they stopped handing down the mutton chop whiskers as part of the inheritance.

And there, finally, came the Councilman with two of the well-upholstered caricatures. These he got along with much better; they didn't intimidate him; those others told him what they wanted and he better damn well go fetch.

They stepped out onto the pavement, paused while one of the corpulent gents lit a cigar, and walked to a limousine at the curb. Miller was hanging back from the Caddy, they weren't taking him along. The chauffeur stood there doing his imitation of a chauffeur in a wax museum, his hand on top of the open back door. One guy got in and the other one, whose back was to the street, was still talking with Miller. Castle fixed all of his attention on Miller's lips. He said, "I can't do it tonight because I got an appointment but I'll get to it right away in the morning."

That seemed to go over all right with the other man because he backed his ample posterior into the car and the chauffeur closed the door on the transaction.

Miller looked after the limousine as it pulled away and then he stepped into the street. Castle slid down on the seat and pushed the hat over his eyes. Miller stepped between the Plymouth and the car in front and Castle saw him through the bullet hole. Christ, he thought, it's kind of corny but maybe I can get a patent and market the hat to other private investigators.

Miller went to the phone booth that wasn't ten yards away. Castle could almost see the numbers the guy was dialling. Miller told whoever it was who he was. The Councilman was sure making this easy. Castle was grateful the fellow had spent half his life making speeches and was thus in the habit of enunciating clearly. He told the person he'd be there at eight and, yeah, he'd be sure to go in the back way.

Miller exited the phone booth and hailed another taxi. The

driver knew him and they exchanged greetings, and Miller said, "City Hall."

He would probably relax in the backseat, digesting his roast beef, inquire about the man's family, and seem real concerned about the brother-in-law with the war wound. He'd promise to do something for the guy, meanwhile assuring himself of another vote for next time, and the time after that. Miller was concerned about the little guy.

Castle decided to take a chance and not tail the cab. There comes a time in this business when you got to play a hunch otherwise you wouldn't be in this business. Of course, he reminded himself, he hadn't been in the business long enough to know if this was true or not but it sounded pretty good.

He went into the phone booth and dialled his own number. He could smell Miller's after dinner drinks on the mouthpiece. He kidded around with Laura and then he asked her to get him an unlisted number. She agreed to do it but he would owe her.

He stood there in the phone booth for five minutes waiting for her to call back. A little man who looked like he spent all day in an office adding up figures in one column and transferring them to another column, came up and wanted to use the phone but Castle told him him he was waiting for an urgent message. The guy gave him a persnickety look and fidgeted like he needed the washroom more than the phone booth. Maybe he wanted to call home and see whether a man answered. Maybe the guy would hire him to find out what his wife was doing while he was at work. Castle returned the man's look and the man went away. Castle was still real tough.

Laura called back with the number. Castle dialled it and all the guy who answered had to say was, "Yeah?"—and he knew his hunch had paid off.

"Sorry, wrong number."

Next he dialled the *Times* and asked for Joe Frontenac.

163

Chapter Twenty-Two

At eight o'clock that evening Castle was behind the wheel of the Plymouth with Joe Frontenac as a passenger and the reporter was looking out the window while he talked. He had been talking without pause since they had met out front of the Press building ten minutes earlier.

"Funny thing is, I know I'm wide awake. I just this moment pinched myself to make sure. We're in your old heap, driving east on Hastings Street. We just passed the Blue Eagle Cafe and the eagle's flapping its wings like it does every night but it still hasn't gotten anywhere. And, hey, there's Two-gun Segal out front of United News. I can recite my membership number in the Newspaper Guild and I remember all the words to God Save the Queen. But you know that song, 'With My Eyes Wide Open I'm Dreaming'? That's how I feel because I do have my peepers peeled, I know you are about to turn right on Main Street and that we are going up to Union Street, but I'm dreaming that we're going to kidnap a prostitute from a whorehouse. Naturally I didn't mention this to old Caleb, that's Carson, my Managing Editor, when he inquired as to my evening's itinerary. *I* didn't think this caper up. It was *you* and you didn't pick *any* old cathouse to grab a prostitute from. Oh, no. The one you pick is run by the biggest gangster in town. A guy who didn't get to his exalted position only because he was smart. No, he got there because he is smart and *mean*. Very mean. In fact, the meanest man in this town and probably any *other* town. Castle, I swear if you're walking me on this, I'll, I'll..."

"You'll what?"

"Well, I won't do *any*thing because I won't be *able* to do anything because most likely I'll be dead. 'He Was There,' is how the head'll read on my obit. And the subhead: 'But He Won't Be Anymore.' A favour you tell me you're doing me. And I say, 'Oh, okay. Aw reet, Pete.' Just like that. I *believed* you, that is the thing I can't figure at all because, as you make this last turn onto Union right here, I suddenly have this sinking feeling, and I have such a feeling for the very good reason that I don't believe you anymore. It's so pretty, isn't it? This corner of Union and Main, and, you know, it never looked quite so good, or any kind of good, before. That store with the olive oil cans in the window, ain't it sweet? And don't you just know they got hot red peppers and strings of garlic hanging from the rafters and barrels filled with olives, and sawdust on the floor? And on the other side, the Chinese places. That one with the red sign and gold letters, you can go in there and they have jars filled with dried seahorses and should a fellow have a hankering for a bear's gall bladder, well, Fong's your uncle. I'd like to be there right now.

"But no, I have to show the girl the pictures and if she identifies the guy, I'm supposed to lead her to the window and out we go. *You* can't go in there because they'll recognize you from the time they beat the b'jesus out of you and threw *you* out the window which happened the day before they serenaded you with machine guns. Yeah, pal, you sure know how to have a good time at a whorehouse. Least you can do is let me show her the pictures *after*."

Frontenac paused just long enough for a dramatic sigh.

"Tell me, Castle; why, really, am I doing this?"

"Why? You know why, Joe. Because you see yourself as all famous daredevil reporters rolled into one. A direct descendant of Billy Russell taking notes as he rode into the valley of death with the Light Brigade. You're part Willy Seabrooke with a little Richard Halliburton thrown in, to be sure, but you're all Joe Frontenac. And, what's more, Joe, you've got printer's ink coursing through your veins."

"Hey, I like that, Castle. Where'd you pick up the style?"

"From reading you, Joe."

"Can you, maybe, give me a little more?"

"Well, let's see. Your heart, your heart beats to the rhythm of the presses thundering in subterranean chambers while a big city sleeps. How's that?"

"Great! I'm rarin to go. Just keep that engine running and get that ladder up to me quick."

Frontenac got out of the car and Castle watched him make a beeline to the door. Now that's the way a fellow is supposed to approach a cathouse. The little slat high up in the door opened and closed and Frontenac passed inside.

Lord, almighty, the reporter exclaimed to himself, I must have interviewed a third of the people in this joint and been at the scene of the arrest of another third. The remaining ones are from out of town. It is just the way Castle described it. Nice, stand up bar, a few tables, some armchairs to make you feel comfortable afterwards and the girls over there inside an enclosure. There's the moon-faced piano player with a disconcertingly sweet and high pitched voice, singing about what to do when romance comes calling.

Say hello to love
Invite it in for a drink
Lay on the hospitality
It's always later than you think

Frontenac got a Billy Rose cocktail from the bar and wandered around the room. He looked right away for the one in the cowgirl attire. She was talking to a doxie in a tight sweater that must be hiding an aluminum-reinforced brassiere. His gaze scampered over the others and rested on the English woman. Maybe the most beautiful woman he had ever seen. But, cool and aloof, sitting by herself in a long gown.

But there was nothing standoffish about the Negress. She came at you like the circus hitting town. All big, brown and rubbery milk chocolate. It was like the Lord above, bless Him, stopped the production line, gathered up the very best of the muscles and bones, tendons and fibres, had a parlay with Himself and declared. "Well it's been a century. I'm gonna do another one who'll be completely outrageous! Hot damn!"

She was out of his league, that was for sure. To even consider it, a man had to be either thoroughly drunk or totally deluded. Or else had to have come down out of the clouds in a chariot with a lighting bolt in his fist and something similar under his toga.

Frontenac himself knew just who he was, and all the Billy Rose cocktails in the place couldn't get him drunk tonight. As for the mythic realms, the closest he'd ever gotten was a press conference in the Cloud Room at the racetrack. Couldn't see himself in a toga, anyway.

Frontenac heard the bell and saw the flag go up in the box, and a woman in a teddy and mules answered the call.

You may be strolling down the Main Stem
Or lost way back in the woods
Driving around in your car
Or stumbling from a bar

167

Frontenac decided he favoured the cowgirl. She was five feet tall and just plump enough with that smooth soft skin. Frontenac had the face of the guy in the chariot but not the stature to match. He was only five-feet six, a fact that was central to his whole life not just his love life. He'd never had any trouble attracting beautiful women—so long as he was sitting down. How many times had it happened? He was in a joint somewhere and a woman gave him the eye. Eventually, he'd have to stand up; maybe he'd have to go to the washroom or maybe he'd be emboldened to saunter over to her, and he'd see her lips part in surprise, the confusion in her eyes as she looked around for the exit. It was the memory of that expression of disappointment that he carried around with him.

> *You're lost at sea*
> *Or out to lunch*
> *Up a creek or playing out a hunch*
> *It doesn't matter cause love don't care*
> *Like those Royal Mounties*
> *It'll find you anywhere*

While giving the joint, his reporter's once over, Frontenac noticed the door to the girls' private staircase open. He could see a man's head, partly obscured by the door's shadow. He called and the Negress stood and went over to him. Wanda did not look pleased when he spoke to her but she went with him. Frontenac observed that a couple of the other girls had been watching and that they traded knowing looks.

He checked his watch. There were ten minutes left to kill so he got another cocktail and brought it to a table by the velvet ropes. His nearest neighbors were a pair of large gents in cheap suits. Frontenac wondered why Castle wanted him to hang around before going up. He wondered where the Negress had gone.

The two guys were having a friendly argument about who

had sold the most farm implements that year. One fellow's neck lopped over the back of his collar. By half falling out of his chair, Frontenac was able to look around the man's massive back and get a look at his pal whose face was like a Christmas ham, with a couple of cloves for eyes. This one said, "Like hell, Gord. You had the better territory is all. You weren't based out of Regina, you couldn't sell cunt to a convict."

He laughed and told his pal to snuggle up to his right fist but he, Gord, was going to *plow* one of those fancy girls before it got too late.

Frontenac had the terrible feeling that one of them was going to decide on the English woman, so he waved his hand at the dwarf who was dressed like a bellhop. The little man took his request to the Italian lady with the moustache. The bell rang and Dolores headed for the door.

"Some fellow got your girl friend, Wally," Gord said. "You going to have to settle for the darkie. Wait'll that gets around back home."

"Yeah, Gord, but it won't make as good a story as you and the legless whore. She's was the only one couldn't run away from you."

Frontenac heard them guffawing all the way past the bar where the dwarf gave the card to the hood who nodded, indicating that he might ascend the stairs.

And the piano player was still singing that song:

> *So like a good boy scout*
> *Don't be caught unaware, unprepared...*

The dwarf escorted him to the door. A tall, gaunt man with black hair was mopping the hallway. Frontenac looked at the janitor, at the dwarf who was walking away, took a deep breath and opened the door.

He had to take another deep one when he saw Dolores

close up. It seemed to him that he uttered a few 'uh's' and 'um's' before managing to say, "So I hear you're from England."

"Yes, that is correct. Do you like English women?"

Frontenac looked past her at the screen and the table that Castle had mentioned. The pitcher and basin were there but no cigar.

"Sure," he said. "I was with the Queen's Own during the War."

Dolores smiled and turned her back to him, looked over her shoulder and pretended to be unable to reach the zipper to her gown.

"Would you be so kind as to help me with this?"

Frontenac obliged, concentrating on his fingers, willing them not to tremble. He was thrilled by every inch of silky skin from the nape of the neck to the small of the back that the zipper revealed. When Dolores began to raise the dress along the scenic route, Frontenac said, "Wait just a second!"

"Yes?" Dolores raised her eyebrows.

"I, uh, met a girl over there. In England. You remind me of her."

"And did you like her very much?"

"I did, yes. Very much."

"Good. Perhaps it will be bring back pleasant memories, then."

She took hold of Frontenac's lapels. He had to look up at her. She seemed to breath faint perfume. Yes, he thought, and I'm going to faint.

"Wait!"

"Again, dearest?"

"I have something to show you first. Some photographs."

"Photographs," Dolores said, calmly. "Why certainly, darling. I would like to see them if they will help to get you in the mood."

"I'm already in the mood."

170

Frontenac reached into his inside jacket pocket, "What these'll do is get me out of it."

"I don't understand."

He took three photographs from the envelope and handed them to her. "Maybe you will."

Dolores looked at the one on top. "What is this?"

Frontenac was surprised. It wasn't exactly an exclamation but she had displayed some emotion.

He gave her a chance to look at the other ones.

"You know that bird?"

"Why, why of course,"she looked incredulous. "But..."

"Who is he?"

"It's Sonny. Sonny Garmano. But..."

"Tell me who he is."

"He's Augie's half-brother. They run this place and a good deal besides."

She reached around back for her zipper, yanked it upward. "Just what is all this about?"

"You don't like them much, do you? You'd rather be back with Skinny, wouldn't you? Just doing special high rollers, eh? And you'd like to get off the pills too, I bet."

"Exactly what is going on?"

"Don't worry, miss. I've come to get you out of here."

"And who might you be?"

"I'm Frontenac of the *Times*."

"There is nothing I want more than to leave this place, I assure you. But don't be absurd. You mustn't play the hero."

She glanced at the door.

"You don't know these people. They would kill us without so much as a second thought."

"We'll be out of here in the time it'd take to get undressed and under the covers. My associate is outside the window now, waiting with a ladder. Take a look. You've met him before, I believe."

Dolores turned from him and went to the window.

171

Her scream and the sharp surprise of it, paralyzed Frontenac for a moment. It was the same feeling as if he'd been
wrenched from a deep sleep; was it the telephone, the alarm
clock, the vice squad, was he dreaming with his eyes wide
open?

Dolores backed away, and turned to him, holding her head
between her hands. The fear in her eyes woke him up and he
was across the room in three strides, looking into Castle's face.
His arms were tied behind his back and his mouth was wrapped with adhesive tape Blood seeped from his hair and down
in a rivulet across his forehead. His left eye blinked as blood
ran into it and his right eye bulged like it was about to explode
from its socket.

Over Castle's left shoulder a gargoyle leered.

Another head, shoulders and finally a gun poked above the
slanting roof. They belonged to the man nearing the top of a
ladder who seemed to shout an order at Castle which was
emphasized by an abrupt wave of the revolver.

Castle took half a step forward and braced the heel of his
left foot against the base that supported the gargoyle. He bent
his knees and was still. The guy barked something at him.
Watching, Frontenac thought maybe Castle was considering
coming the rest of the way in a crouch or else on his knees, and
the guy was probably telling him to get a move on. Hell, Castle, either way, you better do it, you're in no position to bar-
gain. But almost before Frontenac could complete his thought,
Castle brought back his right leg, placed his foot against the
top of the ladder and shoved hard.

The top of the ladder moved away from the roof. Castle
bent his knees even more and his right leg kicked back like a
piston. Even from inside the room with the window closed,
Frontenac could hear the man holler. The ladder swung out,
the hood's gun went off, and he was out there in the wild blue
yonder all by himself, arms and legs flapping and churning like
a character in a movie cartoon who just overshot the cliff.

172

Dolores was peeking through her fingers and trembling; Frontenac was practically having a conniption fit, and there was Castle wasting time looking over the edge of the roof admiring his work.

Castle finally started up the sloped, tin roof, bent over, edging sideways, losing his balance and falling forward, resembling a big, tied-up baby. Frontenac got the window open and reached out to pull him in head first, Castle tumbling down onto the floor. Frontenac ripped the adhesive tape from his mouth.

"Ouch! Oh, man. The hands, untie my hands. There. You should have seen him hit the bricks, almost fell on top of the other guy."

"This wasn't in your pretty little plan." Frontenac had the ropes off. "How do we get out of here now, if you don't mind my asking."

"Hell should I know?" Castle massaged his wrists. "But we can't stay in here. You clue her in?"

Dolores just stared at him with a look of drugged surprise. Castle wondered what they gave her.

"Yeah," Frontenac said.

"Okay. Nothing we can do but try the hall. Let's get going."

Castle opened the door on Augie Garmano, one hand extended forward, the other in his pocket. He was flanked by Vince and Marco. Their hands were also extended, and guns were in them.

"Looks like you either want to shake hands or you were about to come in without knocking. I guess it's the second but that wouldn't have been polite. Also you might have been embarrassed."

Garmano's lips parted and it was like rubble shifting in the bucket of a steam shovel, revealing a line of white marble. He did his impersonation of a laugh. "You're digging your grave with your mouth."

Castle looked at him, at the gunmen.

173

"Maybe I'm just trying to delay the inevitable."

"Yeah. By the way, I kind of expected to find Pasquale and Luigi in there with you. Where they at?"

"Nobody introduced themselves but, Pasquale and Luigi, they must be the guys who aren't so good on ladders."

The travertine disappeared behind the granite.

"Oh, I see," Garmano said, and turned to Vince, "Remind me to fire those two. Give em tickets back."

"Right, boss."

"One of them," said Castle "you better give a ticket on a hospital ship."

"We'll get around to seeing just how tough you are soon enough, gumshoe. You were planning on nabbing the broad, huh?"

"They were not forcing me." It seemed almost as if there was a slight pause between each word. She said it slowly but defiantly.

The boss answered her with a slap across the face. Front-enac made a move toward Garmano who retraced the arc of his swing, hitting the reporter backhanded across the cheek, sending him halfway across the room.

"Madon," said Garmano. "That wasn't nothing. Let's go up to my office. It ain't good for business, me slapping people around practically in the hallway like this. Another thing to think of is, up there nobody'll hear it when people start falling on the floor."

Marco led the parade, Vince behind the prisoners, pointing his revolver, Garmano brought up the rear, hands in his pockets, whistling 'Say Hello to Love.'

A door opened and Marco whirled, quickly for a big man, and levelled his piece on Wally, the ham-faced farm implement salesman from Regina whose hands were doing something in the crotch area. His chins quivered. He grabbed at the buttons with fumbling fingers, urgently, as if the guns were trained on him because he had been caught out in the hallway with his fly open.

Six people stood watching Wally intently, until Garmano said, "How ya doin, pal? Enjoyin yourself?"

Gord pressed himself as close to the wall as he could get and nodded eagerly to convey that indeed everything was swell, mister.

"Fine," said Garmano. "Wonderful."

And the little party continued on to a door at the end of the hall that was marked 'Private.'

They went up stairs to another door and, on the other side of that, a spacious office dominated by a gun cabinet and an ebony desk shaped like a kidney and inlaid with ivory. The carpet was a middle blue colour. On the wall to the right of the door was a map of Italy done in tiles of various colours; on the wall opposite, next to the massive gun cabinet, was a small map of the city of Vancouver and vicinity decorated with tiny red and blue pins. There were half a dozen chairs scattered about the office, each fashioned of chrome tubing and black leather. Two of the chairs were occupied by three people. Councilman Miller sat in one of them; a white man and a brown woman in the other. The man was inside a navy blue uniform with gold braid. Curly white hair sprouted from under his black brimmed, white cap. Most of the woman was outside of her attire which consisted of white lace panties and brassiere.

When the door had flung open, the uniformed man's face was a deep pink colour, probably from the energy expended as he vigorously massaged one of the woman's brown breasts. The woman made no attempt at professional conduct, instead she remained motionless, eyes fixed on the gun rack.

There was another man in there, on the other side of the kidney-shaped desk, his back to the room as he looked out the French windows at the dancing lights of the city.

"What d'you say we all get acquainted," Garmano said. "Gumshoe, you know my man at City Hall, Councilman

175

Miller."

"Yes. It was not a red-letter day in my life when, several years ago, I first met Councilman Miller foreclosing on an aged and infirmed widow."

"It would have been a red-letter day for me, Castle," said the Councilman, "if the aged and infirmed widow had been your dear sweet mother."

"My, my! You do get carried away when there's all this artillery around. Don't you, you pissant?"

"Hey, gumshoe. Watch your mouth, you're talking to a friend of mine."

There was more sarcasm than sincerity in Garmano's voice.

"Some friend, Augie—You don't mind me calling you Augie, do you?."

"No, go right ahead, gumshoe."

"Thanks. Some friend, as I was saying. The guy going all around town today talking about having a big meeting with you tonight."

"What the hell is this?" protested the Councilman.

"Otherwise," said Castle, looking at the boss. "How would I know to be here at eight o'clock? I heard him down on Pender Street. Not very cautious, this friend of yours. This stooge."

Garmano turned his cold dishwater eyes on Miller who held the stare of almost half a second before finding something fascinating on the tip of one of his wingtips.

"What's the meaning of this shit, Augie?" demanded the pink-faced man in uniform. "Bringing this Red in here?"

"This is Chief Wilkins," Garmano said to Castle. He ignored Frontenac.

"It is? I thought it was some customer has to dress up like Captain Cook before he could get his sail aloft."

After he said it, Castle knew what Wilkins was thinking, something on the order of: The creep is going to die anyway, otherwise I'd order somebody to kill him right now.

176

Castle looked from him to the bagman on the other chair to the cement face in a suit, to the tile mosaic map of Italy; looked at the chest with the .30-.30, the .303, one chopped down .22, two sawed-off shotguns, and a Louisville Slugger; at the black desk, and the blue rug, and thought that he would not have picked these surroundings in which to die. No, he would have preferred that terrace in Italy and, if not there, a sunny verandah out in the Okanagan and he'd be willing to settle for only forty more years; but it didn't look as if that was in the cards.

Wilkins was still talking, ranking him. "And no more than a year ago, this bum was over in Africa giving guns to the jigs that were fighting your own people, Augie."

The woman on Wilkins' lap looked away, frustrated, helpless.

"Your boyfriend there; he's got a lot of class, doesn't he, Wanda? It is Wanda, isn't it?"

She nodded her head and moved her shoulders so that her breast got free of the Chief's hand. But he merely snatched it again without acknowledging the woman it came with.

For the first time, Garmano looked at Castle like he merited his full attention. "Is that right? You were in Ethiopia?"

"I'm afraid so."

"Then you and my brother here, have something in common. Eh, Sonny?"

The man at the windows turned around.

Instead of clean, proletarian garb, Alex Tremaine was wearing a double-breasted, Italian-tailored, beige linen suit.

Curious, thought Castle; the guy doesn't stand out as much, dressed this way. He looks like just another handsome gigolo.

"Holy mackerel!"

Castle had nearly forgotten about Frontenac who was at his side now.

"I hope you're memorizing all this," he muttered to the

177

reporter.

Garmano had taken this in, and said, "One of you don't look surprised, learning our little secret."

"What's to be surprised at?" Castle replied. "You think you got secrets? Like I'm not supposed to know you used to be Al Scarbani and you pushed guys off of buildings and bridges, thus earning the quaint sobriquet, 'Pushy'? That's some kind of mystery? Or that you were the big-time mechanic who got the Vice-President of a steel company confused with a card carrying radical and dumped him and then ran to the other side, to Il Duce? In this burg I could round up enough people to make a hockey team, know that stuff. Or maybe you mean the big secret about your name. Garmano, from Garmani. 'This is our secret. This is ourself.' If I recite the rest of the oath will you prick my index finger with a pin and then I'll do the same to yours and we'll play touchy and then I'll be a big mobster and you can send me out on an errand to threaten somebody to sell the family farm to your bagman here? Hey, If I say 'pretty please' will you let me finish the oath?"

"No," said Garmano, calmly like a man taking his time loading a gun. "I'll finish it. 'We show no mercy to our enemies and we strike in the night.' It's night time, wise guy."

"Holy mackerel!"

"Who the fuck's this goofball?" Garmano snapped.

"I'm Fron..."

"Just a pal of mine," said Castle. "He doesn't know nothing about any of this."

"I'm Frontenac of the *Times*."

"You mean, you're the newspaper guy?"

"Yeah, that's me."

"You're proud of that?"

"Yeah. Yes. I am."

"Oh. In that case, just a minute."

Garmano went to the gun cabinet, and took out the baseball bat. He approached Frontenac gripping it a few inches from the bottom.

"It's too bad for you, you told me what you told me," he said. "On account of I was gonna show you a little trick I learned to do with a baseball bat. I was only going to make like Tony Lazzieri across your knees and then I was gonna let you walk out of here. Well, hey, maybe not walk. Crawl, huh? But, now, since I learn you're Frontenac of the *Times*, a big important guy, or, anyhow, a short important guy, and you're proud of being him, then I got to kill you. That way you won't write none of this and I won't have to go to the trouble of bribing a bunch of people to make a show of doing something about it without, naturally, doing nothing. The usual way. But, come to think of it, I can still make like Tony Lazzieri, and kill you after."

Garmano focused on one of Frontenac's knees like it was a hanging curve ball and brought the bat around, stopping it just as it touched the fabric of the reporter's slacks. He smiled at the reporter, and pushed the bat the remaining few inches and Frontenac called out in pain.

"That? That wasn't nothing. That was a bunt. Later, I'll swing for the fences."

Garmano made laughing sounds and they were echoed by Marco. When they were done, Sonny spoke for the first time. "You remember when we met, Castle? I'll give you a hint: it wasn't at the WUA headquarters. It was over dinner, not even three years past."

"I don't need any hints, Sonny. It was at a palace in Addis Ababa. I was seated on the little man's left, and you on his right. You had more nose back then and less chin but the eyes are the same. The little man had been getting small arms from me for months but you were the new supplier of the big stuff. So what if he had to pay you? He needed the things to fight off Viceroy Graziani and his boys. The invaders. He was in good spirits that evening, pleased to have the big guns. He hadn't, however, tried them out yet."

179

"You know, Castle. I didn't like being in prison."

"Our jailors were different, but I didn't either. If you'd given him equipment that worked, Sonny, you wouldn't have landed in jail. There's that to consider."

"I was working for my people, my nation. For Fascism."

"Last I heard Ethiopia and Italy were on different continents. You had it made for a awhile. Partisan gun runner with impeccable, faked credentials. You were real good at infiltrating the enemy camp, eh Sonny? Sell them guns that don't always go bang when they're supposed to, stick for a few days, learn where and when they're to be employed and then run and tell. Only thing is you couldn't fulfill your obligation. Ah, well. The local workingman's more naive than your average Abyssinian freedom fighter. Ripe for the picking. Steal the money, and break the union, so business can proceed as usual. You didn't even have to waste much time preparing your background. Pal of Sacco and Vanzetti, my sweet ass."

"You got a big mouth, you know that?"

"Sure I know it, Sonny. But you got nothing to fret about. Looks like you done all right. Got yourself a new wardrobe. But, I guess, you take your skim from the local rackets, your stipend from the police for inside dope on the pinkoes, and part of twenty thousand, you can buy plenty of fancy threads."

"It gets me plenty other things besides. You want some, you can have it, a guy like you."

"Yeah, Castle," said Garmano. "Maybe we can come to an understanding here. You're a tough bird. Throw you out the window, you walk away. I like a guy like that."

"That ain't nothin, Augie. You should see the way I dodge machine gun fire and roll over and play dead."

"As a matter of fact, I did see. Ha, ha."

Big Marco was right on cue with his own "Ha, ha."

"Augie, you're the only guy I ever met had a hired echo."

"That's good. Hired echo. You'd be a lot of laughs."

180

"So we propose you come in with us," said Sonny. "We need somebody who can get close to the action but who's not of the family."

"Like I said before, I don't like the part where we got to stick pins in each other's fingers."

"Look at it another way. You don't have a choice."

"I looked at it that way already, Sonny. And I don't want any part of it."

"All right, Castle. I respect you but I got to kill you."

"Well, well. Little brother's got big brother around and a couple of hired women, and he's flexing his muscle. You're a regular Gabriel D'Annunzio. But without the heart and the balls. I'll make it easier for you, Sonny. I don't respect you."

Castle was waiting for it but it didn't come from Sonny, who didn't make a move. His brother shot Sonny the look—no rearrangement of facial features, no knotted brows or flashing eyes but it was the look, nevertheless, and as expressive as neon and fireworks. You are an object of loathfulness and disgust, was what the look conveyed. All of this in a split second, the split second before Augie Garmano nailed Castle with a straight right hand that sent him backwards into Marco who pushed him off and slammed a fist into his kidneys. This second blow knocked Castle onto his stomach, and as he rose to all fours, Augie put him back on the floor with a shoe to the side of the jaw.

With the boss turned sideways to him, Frontenac saw his chance and leaped. Garmano merely shoved him toward Vince who hit Frontenac with a left and a right so quickly, the reporter's head didn't have time to move to the left and the right. He was out cold before he reached the Mediterranean blue carpet.

Police Chief Wilkins pushed the woman off his lap, stood and undid the gilt buttons of his coat.

"Let me plug this bum, Augie. For all the bad things he's written about the Force over the years."

"Yeah, sure. Fuck I care," Garmano said, massaging his

knuckles.

Wilkins had just retrieved his revolver when Castle lunged from the floor, clubbing him on the temple. The police chief joined the reporter on the carpet.

"I've always wanted to do do something like that," Castle muttered, and before his legs could give way, he was grabbed from behind by Marco. Sonny came around the desk for the first time.

"I'm going to teach you some respect before I kill you."

He slapped Castle hard across the face.

"That's a warmup."

"Aren't you just a little scared, Sonny? You sure this pithecanthropus man is enough? Maybe you need more guys to hold me, eh?"

Sonny swung his fist this time.

"You don't look so good, big shot. You sure you don't got something else to say?"

Castle's vision was already obscured by the swelling around his eyes.

"Yeah, I do."

The words seemed to blurt out of his mouth, carried on little waves of blood.

"Now I know why I didn't recognize you at the WUA. I never seen you from the front before. In that prison you were always the guy bent over in the showers."

Sonny hit Castle a third time and Castle watched something small and white catapult across the floor. One of his own teeth.

Marco who was still holding him, said, almost in a whisper, "What're you gonna do now, punk?"

Castle knew what he was going to do but he needed a few deep breaths before doing it. Hoping to gain a couple of seconds, Castle groaned deeply which must have seemed reasonable. He thought he heard someone else come into the room, and Sonny's eyes confirmed it.

Castle let out another groan and went limp so that his body was dead weight in Marco's arms. When Marco tightened his hold, Castle reached back with both hands and grabbed at the big man's crotch. He squeezed with all the strength that remained to him. Marco bellowed almost pitifully, and, instinctively, he released Castle who held on until the big man was on the floor. Then he lurched toward Sonny.

Sonny backed away, raising his arms up to protect his face. Castle went under them and to the stomach. it was a good punch but Sonny had been retreating too quickly for it to have much affect. Sonny stopped, came forward with a kick aimed at Castle's groin. Castle had just enough time to pivot and avoid the kick. His back was toward Sonny but he spun and landed his elbow flush on the man's nose.

A voice behind him, cried, "No more! Please, no more!"

But Castle had a little bit more, just a little bit, enough to put Sonny down with blood pumping from his nose.

A shadow came down over Castle's eyes. Something was laid against his throat, a bar or a stick, and someone behind him was pulling back on it. He tried to cry out but nothing came. His breath was leaving him and he couldn't get any of it back. The pain was overwhelming him. He could see nothing. He began to go under, to sink into the indigo sea.

There was a blunt explosion. The pressure lessened and was gone, replaced by a ball of fire in his throat, and another pain, a burning sensation in his arm, just below the elbow. As he struggled to breathe, he heard, behind him, a body fall to the floor. There was a mop at his feet; what's that doing here? he asked himself, as he stared at it dumbly. Looking up, as if for an answer, he saw Augie Garmano, a gun in his hand, his face twisted with hatred.

Finally, Castle turned to see the man on the floor looking up at him, his eyes like broken glass, blood seeping between his fingers from the wound in his side.

"I'm sorry," Emile Lisieux murmured. "But I did not want

183

you to hurt my Sonny."

Castle stared back, uncomprehendingly, holding his arm, swaying, still fighting for breath. He glanced toward Sonny who had risen to his feet but Sonny turned away. Castle decided he didn't know what was going on any longer, and trying to figure it out took too much energy, so he let his body do as it wished. He collapsed onto the floor. The carpet was getting to seem real familiar.

"Enough of this crap." Garmano still had the gun in his hand. "Fun and games are over. I'm gonna start popping witnesses now, beginning with the two broads."

At the boss's command, his two thugs dragged Castle to the chair formerly occupied by the Chief of Police.

"There, you got a ringside seat, gumshoe. I'm saving you for last. It woulda been too bad if I'd a killed you by mistake cause I want you to watch each one of them die. I mean, it's only fair, right? If you wouldn't of come around stirring up trouble, tomorrow they'd all be alive, turning tricks and writing newspaper stories."

"Wait a second, Augie," Councilman Miller spoke. "Perhaps this is getting out of hand."

"When I want to hear from you, I'll ask you a question."

The Councilman retreated and Garmano walked over to where Dolores was sitting.

The point of the barrel of his gun was lost in her thick black hair.

"Bye, bye bitch."

Another voice interrupted him, very loudly. "Drop it!" it said. "All of you!"

Garmano looked toward the sound. Three guns were levelled on him from the doorway. The gun in the middle was held by Detective Lieutenant Koronicki. The cops on either side of him moved into the room.

Garmano did as he was told, the gun emerging from Dolores' hair, clattering against the back of the chair and falling to the floor. But Vince decided not to obey, and went for his piece. Koronicki fired and hit him in the shoulder.

"I mean *no*body move."

The Chief of Police rose from his position on the floor.

"Good work, Koronicki. Just great. I'll take over now."

"Stay right where you are, Wilkins."

"Listen here, Koronicki. I'm your chief."

"Not any more. You're just a two-bit crook to me now."

Koronicki looked away from Wilkins.

"I want all of you over in the corner. I mean move! Murphy, Anstee put the cuffs on them."

Councilman Miller stepped forward, smoothing his lapels and tugging at his cuffs.

"I don't know how to thank you, Lieutenant. I know you'll want my statement. I'm all right so I'll drive myself to the station."

"Corporal Anstee, cuff the suspect."

"Suspect!" Miller stammered, telling Koronicki to see here but, instead, Koronicki looked at Castle who was still in the chair holding his arm and grimacing.

"You all right?"

"Oh, fine. Just fine. I got a hole in my arm, my face probably resembles the blue plate special down at Ramona's, and as I'm telling you how fine I feel, my voice sounds to me like a frog with a hernia. But, what the hell, eh?"

Castle pushed himself up from the chair.

"You fellows sure took your time, didn't you?"

"There were half a dozen individuals downstairs that didn't want to let us come up."

"Thanks, Horace."

Koronicki grimaced, his eyes darted to where his corporals were separating the good guys from the bad.

"I mean, Lieutenant Koronicki. And thanks for not bringing your hot shot partner. With a gun in his hand and me in the picture, an accident might have occurred."

"Just what I was thinking which is how come I sent him to a public school to give the children a talk."

"Yeah, you'll probably get reports about stolen lunch half-brother would find out about us."

"You gave me the clue, Emile. About the two thieves but I didn't get it then. Why did you do that? You must have known it might land all of you in jail."

"'And with Him they crucified two thieves; the one on his right and the other on his left.' I wanted us to go to jail."

His eyes were no longer jagged; the look could no longer reach inside of you and cut at the hidden places.

"In there he would have been different. We would have time together. But now...Now I am going..."

It went out of his eyes and as it did a little smile appeared on his face.

Castle looked up at Koronicki, "Call the morgue."

"Who the hell was he?"

"A French Foreign Legionnaire who thought he was a little Norman nun."

The Lieutenant frowned, "Well, whoever he was, was he one of them?"

"Sort of. 'The scripture was fulfilled which saieth he was numbered with the transgressors.'"

Koronicki shook his head wearily, "Used to be simpler in the old days. You know that, Gene? I miss the old-fashioned murders. Either I'm getting old or it's getting too damned complicated."

"Maybe it's a little of both, Horace."

"You call me that again, I'm booking you."

Castle grinned and went to the French doors, pulled them open and stepped out onto the balcony. He looked down over the sloping, second-storey roof to the alley where two cops stood, the lights of their cruiser cutting red swaths through the night.

Facing the room again, Castle said, "Lieutenant, would you

186

mind if I had a word with Garmano by myself?"

Koronicki searched Castle's face before divesting himself of a plangent sigh. "All I got to say is, I can't be expected to pay attention to everything that's going on, not with all this confusion."

Koronicki turned his back on Castle and resumed barking orders.

"Hey, Pardrone,"Castle called. "Come on over here. Let's have us a little chat."

Garmano levelled the gaze on him. Castle knew what he was trying, the old mal occhio. But it wasn't working.

"Bring him here, will you, corporal? It's Anstee, right?"

"Yes sir."

"Don't worry, he won't hurt me. He's cuffed."

The corporal looked to his chief, who pretended not to notice him. He took Garmano by the arm, brought him across the room and out onto the balcony."

"Fuck is this?"Garmano wanted to know.

"Hey, Pushy. How far you think it is down there to the ground?"

"Why you asking me that?"

"Come on. Look over the railing. Take a guess."

Garmano looked, "Bout forty-five, fifty feet," he mumbled. "What's going on?"

"Well that's not much. Plus, if a fellow went out this window he'd have the edge of the roof below to break his fall. No sweat. I mean, for example, that bridge you pushed old Johnny off of, it must have been, what? Seventy-five, eighty feet? At least, eh?"

"Listen, gumshoe. I didn't shoot you on purpose. The bullet went through the fruitcake and nicked you is all."

The constable was still there and Castle addressed him. "Anstee, maybe you better go see if your Lieutenant needs you."

Garmano suddenly looked like it might be a good idea to

187

follow the cop.

"If Johnny made that, you ought to make this."

Castle grabbed the back of Garmano's coat, bent him for ward over the railing and shoved.

"I'm betting on you, Pushy."

"Mother*fucker!*"

Garmano went down, arms and legs moving like a man who didn't know how to swim but knew he was in deep water. He hit the roof on his shoulder, began to roll and made a futile cuffed grasp for the claws of the gargoyle before hurtling out into space.

Castle stood on his toes for a better look down into the alley. Garmano landed on his side, rolled and came to rest on his stomach. After a moment, Castle saw one of Garmano's hands move in a pool of red neon. His fingers seemed to be clawing at the bricks.

"Tough bastard," Castle muttered. Stepping in from the balcony, he had to move around Frontenac who was seated at the boss's desk, watching him and dialing a number on the telephone.

Koronicki and his boys were leaving the room with Sonny, Wilkins and Marco cuffed and subdued. Wanda and Dolores waited in the hallway. There were four guys in white coats, and two stretchers. Vince went out first. There was still hope for him. The other two hoisted Emile's stretcher, the guy at his head complaining to the other one about having to work overtime and miss Fred Allen on the radio.

"Get me rewrite!" the reporter shouted.

Frontenac held the phone in one hand and rested his battered forehead in the palm of the other.

"Olafson? Yeah, it's me. Stop the presses! Yes, I'm serious. I have to wing it. Ready? Okay, here goes: 'I Was There' by Joe Frontenac..."

Chapter Twenty-Three

His arm was in a sling, his eyes swollen shut, the anvil chorus was at work in his head and clouds hung low over the streets like big Marco about to sit on his chest. Castle felt old; he could look at his birth certificate and do some fancy figuring to prove he was only forty years old but there was no reassurance in that. This damp morning he felt all the other damp mornings, the ones waking in the back of canvas-covered carnival trucks, about a year's worth of mornings in trenches in France, a couple hundred in the steaming Central American jungle, and all those in that pit in Africa where the walls were always wet and they only took away the slop pail once a week.

But he had made all those, and would probably make it again. Louise had hold of his good arm and they were walking down the street and there was Woody up ahead shouting out the news.

"Private Eye Uncovers Biggest Scandal in City History... Read All About It!"

So he had the hole in his arm and another in his hat, and stories in the papers to show he hadn't dreamed it all up, the events of the past week which, as he sat in bed last night, propped up by a pillow, chewing aspirin and pulling on the brandy bottle, he had begun to consider was a possibility. Or, more truthfully, he had begun to hope was a possibility. That if he could only go to sleep, he'd wake up and Louise would be waking up, and they'd play a little slap and tickle, and she'd go off to Seattle with Mandrake, and he could start that morning altogether differently. Maybe he'd head down the block the other way, as he had been tempted to do, go to the track, never show up at the office at all.

"Getchur special edition!...Chief of Police and Head of City Council Arrested...Crime Bosses Nailed...City Hall to Undergo Investigation...Cops and Crooks Conspire Against Organized Labour...Getchur morning paper and read all about it!"

"How about a paper?"

"Sure...Oh, hey! *Mister* Castle. Holy Jeez! You seen this?"

Castle took the paper.

"Here Louise, I can't turn the damned pages. Let's see the sports section."

"You're a hero. Got the whole front page and the two at the centre inside." Woody addressed some potential customers. "Here he is, folks. The man who single-handedly took on the crime bosses. Getchur paper and read all about him."

A couple of men bought a paper and looked at Castle with admiration. Embarrassed, he looked away, fishing in his pocket for change.

"No charge, Mister Castle. It's my pleasure."

"Thanks, Woody but you can cut the Mister routine right now."

"Sure, Gene. Say, you knocked Hitler and the troubles in Spain to the back of the paper."

"What happened with Louis and Schmeling?"

190

"Well, Louis..."

"Who's the two-fisted, ex-soldier of fortune, they're writing about?" Louise interjected. "They couldn't mean you."

She read on, "A life and death drama played out on the top floor of a house of ill-repute as the bells of St. Timothy's tolled."

"Fellow's got a way with words, eh?"

"That ain't the half of it. Listen to how he starts out, 'Fists flew, blood flowed, and guns spit flame in the night. I was there, I'm Joe Frontenac.'"

Thunder rumbled its warning. There was a brief second as Louise, Castle and Woody had a laugh on Joe Frontenac before the rain began its assault.

Woody ducked under the tin roof of his shed, and Castle and Louise dashed for Ramona's Cafe. As they reached the door, the wind grabbed at Louise's hat and coat, and took the newspaper from her hand. The pages separated and went sailing down the street, every page for itself.

There must have been twenty customers in Ramona's, all of them with the morning newspaper, and when Louise and Castle blew in, nearly every one of them wanted to clap him on the back. The pimp and his girl, Maude, Guy Rogers and Raymond Thomas, stood side by side in the greeting line, each in turn telling Castle what a swell fellow he was. Even Tommy Chew looked up from his grille and offered a smile. Captain Matty couldn't get up without a terrible effort so he waved his cane.

Castle and Louise made their way to a booth in the rear where Frank and Finnegan were sitting.

"You really have made an impression," Louise muttered. "Even Beanie Brown's gotten to his feet. And here he comes."

"You read the news, eh?" said the Bean, shaking his newspaper.

"Some of it," Castle replied. "It's pretty embarrassing to tell the truth."

"Yeah," said the Bean. "For you. It's sweet music to my

ears."

"Huh? Whatta you mean?"

"Schmeling. What d'you think I mean?" Beanie Brown unfolded the paper and held it up. The photograph covered half the page. Louis on the canvas, in the process of rolling onto his side, his eyes bleary and unfocused. Yeah, Joe, I know just how you feel, Castle thought. Schmeling standing over him, looking cool and proud, and not nearly as menacing as Augie Garmano.

"You'd a listened to me, Castle. You'd be a rich man this morning. I am."

"Wait for the rematch."

"Who cares? See you, sucker."

Beanie Brown touched the tip of his green visor and walked away.

"Damn, damn, damn," Castle moaned, lowering himself gingerly into the booth next to Frank.

"All this stuff true, Gene?" Frank tapped the paper with the backs of his fingers.

"I'm afraid so. Schmeling by KO in the eleventh."

"Come on, you know what I mean."

"Oh, that. I don't know really. I'm afraid to read it."

"Good morning, folks."

They looked up to see little Joe Frontenac, his hat pushed back just enough that his head bandages were visible.

"You want to know if it's all true," said Castle. "Just ask the man what wrote it. Afterall, He Was There."

"True?" said Frontenac. "True? Hah! Not only is what's there true but I left out some of the best parts to protect the guilty. I mean, the paper made me cut how Chief Wilkins was rubbing the girl's bosom like he was waxing a squad car. And that funny bit when Miller tried to weasel out of it. But the best of all was when Castle shoved the guy off the balcony. 'I'm betting on you, Pushy.'"

Only Finnegan didn't laugh.

192

"Hey, slide over there, will you," Frontenac sat down beside him. Frank brought out a pint bottle of rye.

Finnegan looked up from his coffee cup and cleared his throat.

"Uh, oh," Frank muttered.

"Castle, there is something I have to say to you."

"All right, Finnegan. I'm all ears."

"I believe I owe you an apology."

"You're right, you do. No, seriously, Martin. That is quite unnecessary."

"But it is necessary. And I am sorry."

"Well that's okay. I..."

"Yet I still find it hard to believe that Alex Tremaine is guilty, that he could have tricked us so."

"You'd find it easier to believe," Frontenac said, "if you'd have seen him in his two hundred dollar suit, hitting Castle while that gorilla was holding him."

Finnegan addressed the reporter, "I hope something comes of your story other than the titillation of the masses. I hope next week it's not all forgotten, and that nothing changes but your circulation rate. Yet what else can one realistically expect? You do work for the capitalist press, afterall."

Frank poured some whiskey into Finnegan's cup of coffee.

"Here drink this and relax, at least for this morning."

"You better give him the whole bottle," Louise remarked.

"Sure. Go ahead and have your little joke but nothing has changed for the working people and the poor of this country."

"Maybe it will, Finnegan."

"Maybe is not good enough, Frank. Nothing will be different until power changes hands."

Finnegan raised his cup, sniffed at it, had a sip. "Castle, I wonder what you are going to do now? Have you finally realized the importance of the struggle?"

"Yeah, Gene," said Frontenac. "Now you got enemies in high places as well as the usual low ones. So what the hell comes next? I bet right this morning each one of Garmano's boys who's not in custody, is sipping his morning anisette and plotting how to take over the reins of power. After the new boss emerges, the first order of business will be revenge. Next in line for a piece of your hide is the police department. You only got one friend there but he's only a detective lieutenant. Then there's the legion of land speculators and crooked tycoons and the rats at city hall who'd like to give you a sky-scraper for a tombstone."

"Enough all ready."

"So the point is, Mr. Castle, maybe you ought to disappear for awhile. You thought about that?"

"As a matter of fact, these very things of which you speak did occur to me while I sat up having a wee nip now and again, waiting for dawn to rustle her skirts."

"Pray tell," Frontenac replied in kind. "Did you glimpse wisdom at the bottom of your glass or under those skirts and, if so, did it speak to you?"

Castle looked out the window of Ramona's at the rain that fell like machine gun fire. "I don't know if it was wisdom speaking, Mr. Frontenac. But whatever it was said to me, '*Yo aposto el sol es brillante en Sevilla a este vez del ano.*' Or something like that."

"Hey, that's Spanish. And Sevilla's in Spain."

"That's right, Frank. And there's a civil war heating up, what I hear. It'll probably be back on the front page tomor-row."

"Yeah, yeah, uh huh," Frontenac nodded impatiently. "Now what exactly do you have in mind?"

"I don't know; sort of wouldn't mind having a look. But, what about you, Joe? Muckraking city reporters have a habit of winding up at the bottom of False Creek in cement galoshes. I don't suppose you ever had much of a hankering to be a for-eign correspondent, eh? Guess not. Stay and, maybe in a few years, you'll uncover another scandal."

194

"You kidding?" Frank said. "His brain's working so hard, I can see the bandages wriggling."

"Well, I must admit, there are possibilities to it." Frontenac declared. "I follow you around over there, something's bound to happen."

"Uh huh. And you'd be on an expense account. Plenty to go around. Right old pal, old buddy?"

This time even Finnegan joined in the laughter.

Chapter Twenty-Four

The cab was parked by Pier Eleven at the foot of Shanghai Alley with the engine cut off, the lights still on and the meter running. The fog was so thick that it smothered the light a foot from the hood. Six people stood outside the cab with the rear door opened, and the driver kept looking back there at the rain spattering on the edge of the floor and the corner of the seat. But, what the hell, they were paying for it and they'd been talking for five minutes in the rain. Two of the guys were getting on the ship that rose up behind the Anchor Tavern. When he first drove up, you couldn't even tell there was a ship there, what with the fog and the thin but steady rain. Then the ship's lights came on and they were like stars real close in the night because you still couldn't even see the shadow of the prow or nothing. There must be other cars around and passengers moving from the terminal building to the boat because there was a humming sound, like of conversation and footsteps, and somebody was shouting instructions over a loudspeaker.

Funny, you learn a lot driving a hack and you don't

have to be nosey, asking questions all the time, you just got to look and listen. One of the women, the younger one, although she wasn't that young, closing in on forty, was sweet on one of the two guys in the trench coats who were taking the ship. She wasn't leaving on this trip but even so, she wasn't crying. It was the old dame who was producing the crocodile tears. The old guy, he was even older than the old dame which must put him close to a hundred. Then there was the guy who looked like he spent a lot more time riding in freight cars than taxi cabs. Well it takes all kinds, like Aunt Florence back in Cabbagetown, used to say. But if they were going to stand out there talking much longer, he should ask them if they didn't mind him going over to the Anchor for a couple of pints until they were done.

"Me?" said Frank. "Hell, it's time to head out to the prairies. I'll get back to B.C. for cherry picking time. But, I'll be thinking of you, old buddy. Give the generals and the priests hell for me. And good luck to you too, Joe."

Castle shook his pal's hand, and then gave Johnny a last hug.

"Been nice knowing you, kid," said the old man.

"You sure you're gonna be all right on the stand, Johnny?"

"Yeah, that Finnegan, he'll take care of me."

Rose took a piece of paper from her handbag and gave it to Castle. "This fellow's an old friend of mine. Met him before the war when I lived over there. Runs a cafe in Perpignon. Look him up when you get there. He'll see that you two get through the Pyrenees and over the frontier."

The tears started again and Rose dabbed at her eyes. "Darn it all to hell. Wish I was going with you. You just make sure you come back soon, Gene, and safe."

"Sure, Rose. Can I bring you back something?"

"Yeah, you could bring me back a big hunk of 1911 or 1912. I had them too fast, the last time."

"It's time to leave," said Frank, and he put his hand on the

197

opened door of the taxi. "In we go. No sense catching pneumonia."

The old people got in, Frank after them, closing the umbrella. He shut the door and the driver started the engine.

"Hold on, Bud," Frank said. "The woman'll need a minute."

The driver killed the engine and resumed staring at the raindrops on the windshield.

"You guys better get going or you'll miss your boat. I'll walk with you a second or two."

As Louise took Castle's arm, Frontenac moved off a few yards. He fished a pack of smokes from the pocket of his trench coat, cupped his hands, lit up and made a point of not looking their way.

"Listen, Louise," Castle said. "You can still change your mind."

"What would I do in Spain, baby? I got this chance to go on a big tour of the western states with Mandrake."

She stop walking, "Ah hell, Gene. I'm going back to the cab. We already said our goodbyes."

Louise turned her back to him but before she could take the first step toward the cab, Castle said, "You could go as far as Paris. If you decided to come back, well, we'd of had a week in Paris. You ever seen Paris, Louise?"

Louise started walking away.

She's not going to buy it, he said to himself, and headed for the ship. He caught up with Frontenac who tossed away his butt. Together they hunched their shoulders against the rain and walked faster.

Louise saw the fenders of the taxi, not ten yards away, and she stopped.

"What am I doing?" she said out loud. "I haven't ever been to Paris. A girl hasn't lived unless she's been to Paris, for chrissakes."

Louise turned around and began to run, her heels clicking on the wet dockside.

"Hey, Gene! Frontenac! Wait up!"

Frontenac heard her first, and nudged Castle.

Louise caught up with them, locking on to Castle's arm and pressing close to him.

"But I don't have any clothes. What'll I wear in Paris?"

"Don't worry about that. You'll get a whole new wardrobe when we get there. Charge it to the *Times*, care of Frontenac. He's on expenses."

Louise laughed. Frontenac looked heavenward, and began to emote:

"It was a journey that held all the allure of adventure and romance, and all the dangers of war, as well. It began at the foot of Shanghai Alley and would lead we knew not where. Our ship awaited, looming out of the fog. There was a soldier of fortune, a glamorous showgirl, and me. I'm Joe Frontenac, I was there..."

There was the final blast of the ship's whistle, and they ran for the ramp.

The cab driver drummed his fingers on the steering wheel.

"I'm beginning to get the idea, the dame's not coming back."

"Yeah," Frank smiled. "I think you're right. Let's go."

199

PRINTED AND BOUND
IN BOUCHERVILLE, QUÉBEC, CANADA,
BY MARC VEILLEUX IMPRIMEUR INC.
IN MAY, 1997